THEIR LITTLE LIES

QUINN AVERY

MYSTERY, SUSPENSE, & THRILLER
WRITTEN AS QUINN AVERY
www.QuinnAvery.com

BEXLEY SQUIRES MYSTERY SERIES
The Dead Girl's Stilettos
The Million Dollar Collar
The Guard's Last Watch
The Skeleton Key's Secrets
The Notebook's Hidden Truths
The Neighbor's Dark Past

STANDALONE ROMANTIC SUSPENSE/THRILLERS
What They Never Said
In Her Father's Shadow
Woman Over the Edge
Deadly Paradise
Lost Girls of Kato
Moscow Mules & Murder
Right Across the Bay
Their Little Lies

CHILDREN'S BOOKS
WRITTEN AS JENNIFER NAUMANN
bit.ly/dogsdonthavefins

Dogs Don't Have Fins
Dogs Don't Have Antlers

PRAISE FOR RIGHT ACROSS THE BAY

"RIGHT ACROSS THE BAY is an enthralling thriller with more than its fair share of twists and turns. Quinn Avery displays a knack for hooking in her readers right from the opening paragraph, blending moments of ripe romantic intrigue with high-tension thrills."
-IndieReader.com

"A small town murder mystery that is anything but small. Right Across the Bay is a must-read whodunnit infused with romance, betrayal and an unforgettable finale."
-BestThrillers.com

"Without a doubt one of the best thrillers I have ever read, I devoured this in one sitting literally unable to put it down. An incredible gripping, unpredictable read full of secrets and twists. An absolute must read."
-ericas_bookreviews

"I absolutely loved this book, it was a really quick and easy read. I found it engaging, fast paced and hooked me straight in"
-joebella_p_reads

"This one took me by surprise more than once. I was not expecting the culprit at all and had a couple of jaw-dropping moments as I read."
-2manybooks2littletime

Their Little Lies
1st Edition
Copyright © 2024 by Jennifer Naumann
Cover: Najla Qamber Designs
ISBN: 979-8-9906697-0-3
Library of Congress Control Number: 2024916280
www.QuinnAvery.com

For my badass friend, DeDe

PROLOGUE

The girl was acutely aware they were running for their lives as they darted barefooted through the forest. If they dared to stop, they would die. She was sure of it. At least as sure as any 6-year-old could be.

Although her parents didn't allow her to watch horror movies, she knew he intended to hurt them in a bad way. A way from which they would not recover. She had seen her share of movie trailers with monsters like Freddie Kruger and Jason Vorhees to understand this was The End. They could not outrun him. The way he remained close behind no matter how fast they ran, she was convinced he possessed an extraordinarily inhuman power, just like Freddy and Jason.

There would be no escape.

The girls clutched each other's hands as they navigated

through the dense trees. Matching braids, one golden blond and one tawny brown, slapped against their backs with every stride. It was a cool summer evening, cold enough to warrant a sweatshirt or a light coat. Their skin pricked painfully with goosebumps beneath the identical flannel pajamas her friend's mommy had sewn.

With thoughts of her friend's mommy, tears sprang from her eyes, and snot filled her sinuses. Fire and bile blazed up her throat. Her friend's mommy was the most gentle person she'd ever encountered. She baked them gooey chocolate chip cookies and helped them make fun crafts. She played dress-up with them sometimes. Bought them Barbie dolls and accessories from the thrift store that were in near-perfect condition. The vision of the kind woman lying still on the floor, blood smeared across the corner of her slack mouth, was more horrifying than the girl could take. She wanted to curl into a ball and cry herself to sleep.

The rigid weeds stung like little needles against the pads of their feet. The aroma of a campfire penetrated the darkness from a bonfire nearby. She wished she was home in her bed instead of blindly running through a forest with the man yelling after them.

Beyond the frantic huffs of their breaths and the snap of fallen twigs beneath their feet, the pounding of his footsteps behind them were the only sounds to be heard.

Something deep down inside the girl pushed her to keep going.

She could finally see the road she was certain they came in on when her friend tripped over a branch and fell forward. She tried to help her crying friend back to her feet, but it was too late. He had caught up to them.

With one fleeting glance at the feral look in his eyes, the girl could not move. Her brain commanded her feet to run, but they remained motionless. Although her lungs longed for air, they would not fulfill their duties.

His eyes narrowed on her little friend. "What did you see back there?"

She was too young. Too sweet. Too innocent.

"Close your eyes," the girl told her friend.

The girl braced herself, flinging her arms out at her sides, making herself as big as possible to protect her best friend from harm. Just then, the dark shadow of another person appeared behind him. Was it someone who had come to save them or someone who wanted to help him? Could it be her mommy?

Next thing the girl knew, a knife pierced her without a sound, cutting through her skin with the ease of melted wax.

Shock rattled her to her core. She didn't believe anyone would actually hurt her or her friend.

All at once, her head became lighter than air. Pain sliced through the knife's point of entry, excruciating and deep.

Another stab of pain rippled through the girl.

She closed her eyes and slipped into darkness with the ease of going to sleep.

CHAPTER 1
PRESENT DAY

Josephine

A dull pain begins to throb against the base of my skull as I pull into the driveway of my childhood home in Ames, Iowa. There's nothing unordinary about the quaint neighborhood or the two-story bungalow I was raised in.

At least from the outside.

In the past several decades, the original 1970s brick accents and windows have been replaced, and the wood siding has been updated with white vinyl. Keeping the yard, landscaping, and the house's facade in pristine condition has been a side hobby of my dad's for as long as I can remember.

It's what happened within the walls of the house that churns my gut.

Since Diane's—my mother's—unexpected death in my early 20s, my visits to Ames have lessened more and more with each passing year. While I've never been particularly close with my dad, I figured it was time to return as he's in bad shape after complications from a dental surgery, and the house could most likely use some upkeep.

It was also a foolproof excuse to leave the station for a while and clear my head after neglecting to properly close two related homicides. The black mark on my nearly perfect career was enough to make me consider an early retirement. My Lieutenant was gracious enough to allow me as much time as necessary to "get my dad's affairs in order," even though I suspect he knew the real reason for my requested leave. In hindsight, failing to pin two murders on a woman suffering from mental health issues was a rookie mistake. Maybe it's a sign that I'm past due to hand in my shield and service weapon.

I let my Australian Shepherd out of the car and

reluctantly shuffle toward the landscaping to rummage through a patch of rocks in search of the hidden key. Behind me, my dog does his business on the lawn, perfectly trimmed to Frank Kelly's standards. I have no idea who my dad hired to tend to the yard after he was sent to the nursing home, but part of me hopes Henry kills a decent section of the grass with the runs he tends to get after long car rides.

"Can I help you?" a deep voice booms with irritation from behind me.

Spinning around to defend my actions, I'm confronted head-on with the most significant chapter of my past.

Rocco Giordano.

A disconcerting blend of buried emotions re-emerges as we simultaneously take a second to acknowledge each other. My childhood friend has changed significantly since our last encounter. The bulky frame he earned from lifting weights in his teens and beyond has smoothed into leaner muscle mass. His cheekbones and strong jawline are more prominent with the transition as well. His expressive eyebrows, neatly trimmed beard, and dark hair—significantly longer than I've ever seen—have become threaded with silver strands. Faint crow's feet surround his black-as-coal eyes, and a set of elevens accentuate the bridge of his intense nose. The only things to remain the same are his olive skin tone from his Italian heritage and his beautiful, full lips.

I'm nearly knocked off my feet when recalling the power behind those fantastic lips.

Our eyes lock. His eyebrows rise, and his mouth gradually quirks with a grin. I try not to imagine what kind of changes he sees in me. When I rolled out of bed this morning, I slapped my strawberry blond hair into a high ponytail and threw on a pair of joggers with an oversized hoodie.

Although I stay in shape as much as my demanding schedule will allow, I've packed on some weight in my lower gut, and my skin is beginning to sag in baffling places. It's so unfair how men naturally become more attractive with age while women frantically search for the right creams, gels, and supplements to retain any resemblance of their youth.

"Jo! I can't believe you're here!" With a beaming smile, he removes his left hand from his tan cargo pants. My eyes catch on his bare ring finger when he waves said hand, inviting me in for one of his legendary hugs. "Get over here, you!"

"Hey, Rocco," I reply with a weak smile and an awkward step closer.

There was a time I would've sprung into his embrace and buried my face against his worn-in ARMY t-shirt to inhale his familiar scent. I spent the better part of three years encased in the comfort of his arms. But it occurs to me that Rocco is one of few people alive who knows the reason I don't like to return home. A strong urge to retreat inside without saying anything more seesaws down my spine.

The truth is, I want nothing to do with Rocco Giordano.

Before I can slip inside his waiting arms, a wiggling mass of merle fur darts in between us. I reach for Henry and miss, expecting him to start the usual protective growling bit he does when introduced to a strange man. Instead, he scales Rocco's muscular legs, eager to lick his face.

"*Down*, Henry!" I scold, successfully hooking my fingers beneath his collar.

"He's a sweetheart," Rocco comments with a good-natured chuckle. "Beautiful coloring, too."

"He's usually better behaved." I squat to sink my

fingers into Henry's thick coat, finding comfort in the gesture. "He seems to like you better than most men."

His grin deepens. "What brings you back to Ames?"

"My dad had a bad reaction to anesthesia, and he isn't doing so well."

Rocco nods impatiently. "I know. I've been caring for his yard ever since he was moved to the nursing home."

I try my hardest not to react even though his misguided loyalty to my dad stings. When we were kids, Rocco *always* had my back. I was under the impression that he hated my old man as much as I did back when I wasted my time and energy giving him any thought.

His brows scrunch together. "That happened *months* ago, Jo. What brings you here *now*?"

My family's dark secrets weigh heavily in the crisp October air as his dark eyes bore into me, awaiting my answer. He knows damn well I don't care what happens to my dad.

"*You're* taking care of the lawn?" I ask, giving Henry one last pat on the head before returning to my feet and regaining my composure. I gesture to the longer hair slightly curling above his ears.

"You've clearly retired from the Army. Are you living around here?"

"I've moved home, actually." With a sheepish look, he combs a hand through his thick hair, causing some of it to tumble over his forehead. I'm abruptly transported back in time, recalling the handsome 22-year-old who told me he was leaving to join the military. "I started caring for Nonna after Papá died a few years back."

A pang of sympathy stabs my heart as I touch his arm. His dad had been a kind, hard-working man who had been there for me at critical times when my parents had not. I may not be close with my dad, but Rocco could've given me the courtesy of letting me know his dad had passed away. "Oh, Rocco. I'm sorry to hear that. What happened?"

"He had an aneurysm. Died during open heart surgery." He reaches up, wrapping his hand around my wrist. My heart trips into an erratic handful of beats with the electric warmth of his skin on mine. "They gave him a proper veteran burial with the twenty-one gun salute and everything."

I squeeze his bicep. "He was so proud of you, Rocco."

"He loved you, you know. Shortly before he died, he called me a bonehead for not dragging you along and making you my wife when I left for Fort Moore."

"He never quite grasped the idea of a woman becoming a cop," I tease. We exchange equally sad smiles before I drop my hand from his arm. "I suppose I better head inside and assess the damage."

"It shouldn't be too bad," he tells me. "The cleaning service stops by every other Thursday, and I saw their van leave the driveway yesterday." With a hesitant pause, his gaze skips over to my front door. "Did you stop for dinner on the way down?"

Although I haven't had anything to eat since early this morning, and my stomach rumbles with the mere mention of a meal, I need to end this unbearable reunion. "Henry was locked inside the car for three hours and needs to stretch his legs. He has an insane amount of energy—his last owners couldn't deal with it, so lucky for me, they dropped him at the shelter." I shrug. "I'm going to order something in."

Rocco winces and gives a shake of his head like I've announced I'm ordering cyanide. "There's leftover tortellini in brodo back at my place. Nonna barely eats anything these days…it'll take a week for me to finish it by myself. I'll heat it up and bring some over."

The gnawing urge to withdraw and put more

distance between us deflates with the mention of his Nonna's famous dish from Bologna. "Damn it, Roc. You know I can't say no to that."

And now I'm calling him by the name I used when we were in love. Double damn it.

He eyes my vehicle. "Do you need help carrying anything inside first?"

"I can handle the one little bag I brought," I explain. "I'm only staying the night."

Disappointment briefly flashes through his eyes before he catches himself and throws me a flirty wink. "In that case, we better hurry and catch up before the night's over."

As he walks away, I begin inventing plausible excuses to end the night early.

———

After washing and drying the dishes, we head into my dad's backyard and settle in lawn chairs around the fire ring. The yard behind the house seems twice as small, but I suppose the feeling is expected when a grown adult returns to their childhood home.

It's a pleasantly warm fall evening, the kind in which a person could stay up all night and remain comfortable in jeans and a sweatshirt. Stars twinkle far above the mostly quiet neighborhood, save for the chirp of crickets and the faint roar of a few college kids in one of the rentals down the street.

Since my dad only partially replaced the 5' fence separating our house from Rocco's, the small hole I'd once communicated with Rocco through remains. Stomach lurching with the dark memories that hole resurfaces, I take a deep breath and inhale the lingering scent of burning leaves.

My childhood was so messed up.

Rocco had thrown Henry the ball so many times during dinner that my dog lazily stretches out on his back with a comical groan.

"I don't think I've ever seen him this tired," I comment before chugging the remainder of the wine Rocco brought with dinner. I stand and give the house a quick glance. As much as I don't want to spend the night in my old bedroom, it'll burn less than revisiting my history with Rocco. "I suppose I should set up his kennel and let him settle in for the night."

"Eager to get rid of me already?" Rocco asks with one brow raised.

I raise a brow back at him. "Do you want me to be honest?"

"Absolutely."

Our gazes lock over the fire's flames licking the sky between us. "Being with you makes me…uncomfortable. I've never told anyone about the messed up things my parents did when I was a kid, mostly because it's something I've tried like hell to forget. You and your dad were the only two who knew, and I technically never told you, either."

"Nonna knows," he reminds me with a bob of his head. "But neither of us would tell a soul."

Something inside me cracks a little with the empathetic expression etched on his face. "If I'd known you moved back, I probably wouldn't have made the trip down."

"Is this old mug that difficult to look at?" he teases, scratching his beard.

"You know what I mean."

"I guess I don't." With a huff, he sets his empty wine tumbler on the ground and stands, rubbing his hands together. "I'm sorry I make you feel that way, Jo. I was so damn excited when I found you in the yard. It was almost like no time had passed since we stood in the same spot and said our last goodbyes. I didn't imagine we'd go this long without seeing each other again. I was looking forward to hearing what you've been up to these last couple of decades. Since that clearly isn't going to happen, I'll show myself out. But first, there's something I want to give you."

I grind my teeth together as he approaches me with a cautious expression. A fury of memories, both good and bad, unleash as he hovers over me, too close for my comfort. The teenage girl lingering deep down longs to drag him close and rekindle the love we once shared. The wiser, more experienced part of me wants to shove him back and run.

My heart races when he extracts a plain square envelope from his back pocket.

Please don't let it be a love letter.

"Your dad asked me to pass this along to you after he's gone," he explains. "I don't have any idea what's inside, but I thought maybe you'd like to take it home with you." His Adam's apple bobs with a hard swallow. "In case we don't ever see each other again."

He nudges the sealed envelope inside my hand and presses a firm, lingering kiss against my forehead. I subtly breathe in his scent, committing it to memory. A turbulent rush of tears stings my eyes as he bends to rub Henry's head before disappearing inside, presumably to retrieve the clean pasta dish.

Legs weak, I lower to the ground beside Henry

and bury my face inside his thick gray coat spotted with black, letting the fur absorb my tears.

I've always wondered if Rocco Giordano could've been my soul mate, if I were to believe in that kind of thing. It's a moot point since I can't afford to let myself feel vulnerable around anyone anyway. My future as a worthwhile detective is already under question.

Blinking back lingering tears, I sit upright and rip open the envelope. There's a Polaroid inside and nothing else. *Odd.*

In the faded photograph, two little girls look straight at the camera, hands held between them. One of the girls is blonde, while the other one is brunette. There's a slight difference in their height, probably because the brunette appears to be a year or two older. Both have beautiful chocolate brown eyes, and their facial features are well-balanced, possibly due to a mix of European ancestries. They wear identical sundresses in a green and white print, with their hair styled in matching French braids.

At first, I think I'm imagining things when I see my reflection in the blonde, as it's getting darker and I've started using reading glasses. Then I squint and hold the Polaroid a little farther away to confirm it's true. But that can't be right—I was a brunette throughout my childhood. My journey to becoming a blonde was gradual, starting when I left home and followed the 1990s trend of chunky highlights.

I don't recognize the brunette.

I flip the picture around, expecting to find a date or the girls' names.

Written in shaky, block-style handwriting I recognize as my dad's are the words, *"I'M SORRY."*

CHAPTER 2
BEFORE

Rocco

A new family is moving into the house next door. I drag a bar stool to our kitchen window and watch closely as a big white truck parks in the driveway of the empty house. I prayed in the night for them to have a son my age. Our neighborhood is filled with old people like Nonna who only want to play stupid card games.

There are only so many ways I can play G.I. Joe by myself. Nonna gets sad when I leave her home alone for too long, so I don't really have many friends. The few I have usually only hang out with me at school because they live too far away from our house to ride our bikes. Nonna doesn't have a license, and their parents are either busy with their other kids or work weird hours. Every now and then, when I get invited to a birthday party, my friend's mom or dad will give me a ride.

I hold my breath when the truck's passenger door opens. A little blonde girl in white jeans and a rainbow sweater darts inside the house through the front door. She runs so fast that I barely see her face. It's not long enough to guess her age. Letting the air out of my cheeks before holding my breath again, I press my nose against the window and wait for a boy —or two—to exit behind her. I wouldn't really care if they weren't my age. I'd even settle for a teenager.

Nonna has frilly junk all over the house. The hand soap she buys smells like roses. Her towels are pink. The dishes we eat on are covered in a yellow flower print. Sometimes I walk into the bathroom to see her underwear drying on the shower rod. I'd give up my Jabba the Hutt lunchbox for a chance to hang out with any other boy for more than a handful of hours every week.

Disappointment settles in my bones when a mom and a dad are the only others to leave the truck.

How dumb.

"What are you doing?" Nonna asks in thick Italian. "It's not polite to spy on others."

"I'm not," I reply in English, hopping down from the kitchen stool. "I'm watching for rain. It's cloudy out."

Nonna has been in the States since I was born and still refuses to learn English. She moved here permanently from Bologna after my mamma died giving birth to me, and Papá had to return to his post in Germany. Most of the time, it's just the two of us.

Sometimes, Nonna cooks at my aunt's Italian restaurant in downtown Ames, where my momma worked before I was born. I sometimes go with her to bus tables and hang out with my older cousins in the summertime.

I know it bothers Tita when Nonna won't communicate in English with the other employees because I've heard her yelling at Nonna a bunch of times about it. I don't understand why she's too stubborn to learn the language. I keep hoping that if I refuse to speak to her in Italian, she'll eventually learn *something*.

Nonna shuffles over to my spot at the window and presses her hands against her hips. She's the type of grandmother who's really short, looks squishy, and gives suffocating hugs. Since I never got to meet my mamma, my connection with Nonna is extra special. She pretty much raised me by herself since Papá has only been home a few months since my fourth birthday. The only time I'm actually glad she doesn't speak English is when she calls me "her baby boy" in public. *How embarrassing.*

"That man has shifty eyes," she reports, stopping to give a disapproving click of her tongue. "And the woman…she looks hard. Not friendly. I do not think I like them."

"I thought you said it's rude to spy on others," I remind her, laughing when she merely rolls her eyes and gives another sharp click of her tongue. I'll probably never know if she understands half of what I say.

"You go over there, make friends with that girl," Nonna instructs me. "I see her there in the backyard. She does not look happy to be here. Invite her over for some of my cannoli."

"No way," I reply. "She's *a girl.*" When I click my tongue and roll my eyes, Nonna gives me a stern look. I guess she's the only one who can get by with that attitude in this house.

"Okay, fine," I grumble, thinking of all the ways my life is totally unfair. Why couldn't my parents have had other kids before my momma died? Why can't Nonna and I move to Germany with Papá? Nonna says it's because Papá has a very important job in the military and doesn't have time for us, but whatever. It's not like I'm a baby and need a lot of attention. It'd just be nice to see him more than a couple of times every year. I'm the only kid in my class who doesn't have either a mom or a dad at home. Some older kids like to tease me for being an orphan, even though it technically isn't true.

I take as much time as possible before heading outside, stopping to tie and retie my sneakers, straightening the rug the way Nonna likes, and studying the creaky door as I move it back and forth like I'm wondering the best way to fix it.

I'm not shy. Not really. I talk to the other third graders just fine. So I don't really know why I don't want to go over to meet the girl, except I don't. I didn't even get a good look at her. What if she's like that one guy in *The Goonies*, with a messed-up face and a need to be chained to the wall? Honestly, I never watched the rest of that movie after that scene. I figured it was way too scary for someone my age.

Grabbing my basketball from a shelf in the garage, I lob a few shots at the hoop on wheels Papá gave me on his last visit home. I usually only play basketball when forced at school in phy-ed class. I hate the sport and can't ever get the ball to land anywhere near the net. Plus, I think my Papá bought a hoop made for babies because I can almost touch the bottom of the net. It's still better than going over to meet the new girl. I'd rather have to complete the Presidential Fitness Test ten times in a row than go over there.

I keep an eye on the house next door, watching the mom and dad move boxes into the house for what must be an eternity. The girl doesn't come outside again. I guess she's one of those spoiled types, like Sara Duncan at school. Whenever it's her turn to do something in the classroom, she pretends to be sick or bribes one of the other kids with candy so they'll do it for her.

I hate this girl already.

Before long, the sun sinks behind the big maple tree above me, and the parents seem to have the truck completely unloaded. Right when I'm ready to give up and head inside, I hear whimpering from their backyard. Figuring they brought a dog that I somehow missed seeing them take out of the truck, I head over to the fence between our backyards. There's a hole at the far end of the wall. It's kind of hidden by one of our wild bushes, so I'm not sure anyone else knows it's there. I once used it to spy on the last neighbor lady while she was sunbathing. After the gross things I saw, you'd think I'd know better than to look through that hole again, but I guess I don't.

The new girl sits on the ground with her arms wrapped around her bony legs, long yellow hair spread around her knees like a curtain. She's pretty small, so I think she's really young—like *preschool* young. After a few seconds, I realize the whimpering sound is coming from her. She's crying.

Oh great. Nonna will probably make me volunteer to babysit the little brat.

"Hi," I call out to her. "I'm Rocco. I live next door."

Her head jerks up. When her big brown eyes lock on mine I decide she's pretty cute for a kid her age. Maybe we could hang out sometime. She could be the little sister my parents couldn't give me. I suppose it would be better than hanging out with Nonna all the time.

The girl stares back at me, her face blank. *What if she speaks Italian, like Nonna?*

I attempt to introduce myself again, this time in Italian. She only blinks back. *Maybe she's deaf.*

"What's your name?" I yell, switching back to English.

She blinks slow and hard until fresh tears spill down her thin cheeks. She's tiny, like a hummingbird.

"It's okay to be sad," I say. "I would be sad, too, if my Nonna made me move to a different house. You can come hang out with me and Nonna sometime if you're lonely. Her English isn't the best, but she's nice and she wants you to come try her cannolis. She moved here from Italy when I was a baby, and she's the best cook around. Maybe you can come join us for dinner sometime."

The girl remains silent. Maybe she's embarrassed that I saw her cry. Or maybe she's just really, *really* shy, and her parents taught her about Stranger Danger. I guess it would be fair because she doesn't know me.

Giving up, I throw her a little wave. "Great talking to you. Guess I'll see you around."

As I round back to the front of the yard, the parents are huddled on their front doorstep, whispering back and forth in sharp voices like they're mad about something.

The man is tall with jet black hair, like my Papá, and wears a pair of windbreaker pants with a ratty old sweater. His eyeglasses have clear frames with thick lenses and his hair is neatly parted down one side. I can picture him wanting to throw a ball around the backyard. What if he wishes he had a son? Maybe he could be a father figure to me while Papá is away.

The woman is nearly as tall as the man and almost sick-looking skinny with curly brown hair the color of tree bark. She wears a dress printed with rusty-colored flowers that's really ugly. Red circles around her dark eyes make them puffy like Tita's get whenever she talks about my momma.

They stop talking when they catch me staring.

I clear my throat. "Hello, ma'am." I nod at the dad. "Sir. My name's Rocco. I live right next door with my grandma."

Behind his glasses, the dad's green eyes flash bright with kindness. "Hello, Rocco. It's very nice to meet you, son."

"Would it be okay if your daughter came over to my house? My Nonna made cannolis and—"

"She's not *our daughter*," the woman snaps at me, her eyes suddenly as dark as the sky gets in the middle of the night.

Whoa. Maybe they aren't as nice as I thought.

Shuffling back a little, I point at the fence. "Then who is she?"

The dad, or whoever he is, grabs the woman's

arm and leans in to whisper something into her ear. I glance at our house, hoping Nonna's watching out the window. Maybe she'd decide to come over and save me from whatever is going on with these weird people. Although the light over our stove is on, the rest of the kitchen looks empty. *Dang it.*

Finally, the woman jerks away from him and shuffles into their house, walking funny, like she's got a hitch in her side. I let out a shaking breath.

What was that about?

"I'm sorry, sir," I tell the man. "I don't know what I said—"

"It's been a long day," he explains with what Nonna calls "a plastic smile" spread over his lips. She says people do that because it's expected, not because they're nice. "My wife is just upset with our daughter after the long ride here. It was good to meet you, Rocco. Have a nice night."

I quickly turn around and run back home, only glancing at the fence. I don't plan to start another conversation with the adults anytime soon. However, that doesn't mean I can't keep trying to get to know the little girl. Nonna is right, she doesn't seem happy. Maybe I can be her friend.

CHAPTER 3
PRESENT DAY

Josephine

After Rocco leaves me with the envelope, I grab my readers from my duffel bag and sit at my parent's ancient oak table in the dining room. With Henry curled up at my feet, I continue to thoroughly study the Polaroid of myself with different colored hair, standing beside a girl I don't recognize. Was the girl a cousin? A friend? The only identifying mark I'm able to find on her is a small birthmark above her right eyelid, shaped like a clover without a stem. It's pretty weak, especially as some kids outgrow birthmarks with time, but it could be something to work with.

For someone who doesn't fully comprehend the science behind graphology, I spend far too much time examining my dad's diminished handwriting on the back. What could he possibly be sorry about? Why did he want me to have the picture *after* he died? Did he have an affair with another woman? Was the girl a secret he kept from my mother? Why don't I remember her?

The thing bothering me the most is what reason would my mother have to bleach my hair at such a young age? She didn't believe in spending money on frivolous things. She wore her hair naturally curly and cut it herself on the first Sunday of every month. I remember it all too well because she'd make me stand behind her with a handheld mirror the entire time. More importantly, why am I a brunette in every other photograph I've seen of myself as a child?

Any memories I retained before the age of seven or eight have dissolved with time. My parents said we lived in their home state of Arizona before moving to Iowa, but I've never been able to recall our home before coming here. I don't have any general visions stored away of the desert. The only glimmer of recollections I've retrieved that could possibly have happened before coming to Iowa are associated with voices, smells, or a fleeting sensation. Certainly nothing that makes any sense. My clearest, unshakable memories begin several years after we relocated to Iowa.

My mother passed away long before I fully understood the gravity of the situation. It was before I started my training at the police academy and began cataloging the important questions that needed answers. As I watched her take her last breath, I was filled with regret for not confronting her earlier. The regret was so consuming that I didn't feel any sadness when she passed away.

My dad became withdrawn after her death. And now the doctors say he's severely incapacitated after a stroke that likely caused irreversible brain damage.

I alternate between wanting to scream and laugh myself into hysterics. My childhood was shrouded with horrible secrets and unsolved mysteries. What's one more?

My head's spinning by the time I decide I've analyzed the photograph to death. Fortunately, Dad still keeps the cupboard above the refrigerator well stocked with alcohol. I pour myself a short glass of whiskey on ice and head into the living room, deciding it's time to let my professional instincts take over. I scan the room, assessing it like a crime scene.

Not much of anything appears to have changed since I left home at the age of eighteen and Diane's death a handful of years later. Although the house had been remodeled around that time, the deep red accent wall and gold curtains adorned with flowers the same red as the wall show their age. Considering it was a pet-free home, I'm not exactly surprised to discover the nylon berber carpet shows almost no sign of wear. The garish couch and matching armchair, a shade lighter than the curtains, don't appear to have been used much either.

My dad's 1980s recliner is the only piece of furniture showing signs of use. The rose-colored arms and headrest have become threadbare with regular use. At some point, he replaced the old console television with a thick flatscreen that's now 10-15 years outdated.

Beneath a metal cross and a portrait of a caucasian Jesus, my mother's hideous collection of porcelain clowns still occupies an entire curio cabinet in the corner. Dad must've instructed the cleaning staff not to bother with them as the shelves are covered in thick dust. It wouldn't be for sentimental reasons because that's not an emotion my dad ever displayed, so it must've been to save on the cleaners' time.

The set of red-spined encyclopedia books Dad sold before we moved here fills an entire side of the built-in bookcases surrounding the wood-burning fireplace. Although the brick firebox is stained with soot, the cubby for firewood is empty. My mother loved the ambiance of a fire on a cold winter night. Dad hated the inconvenience of buying chopped wood and bringing it home. I don't imagine he ever started a fire again after Mother died.

Photo albums and classic novels fill the remaining built-in shelves. I bet if I were to thumb through each book, there'd still be a loose sticker on wax paper jammed next to page 55 of every one. I conducted a test around the time I was thirteen, convinced my parents had never read a single book on that shelf and Diane had only purchased them for show. I found it to be peculiar, considering we rarely had company.

Snagging Hemingway's *The Sun Also Rises* from the shelf, I decide to test my theory. I skip to page 55 and find a scratch-and-sniff sticker featuring an illustration of a pickle with googly eyes. To amuse myself further, I scrape my nail against the sticker and catch a whiff of its lingering scent. I toss the book onto the floor and page through more novels, finding more of the same. Some remain stiff with newness, and the glue crackles with the turn of every page.

I glance at the pile I've made on the floor, dumbfounded. While Diane may have read the books when she was younger, I don't understand the need to display new copies. It shouldn't surprise me that I don't understand her actions because I never did.

After slugging back the rest of the whiskey, I sit cross-legged on the carpet and grab the first photo album. Henry settles in next to me, resting his chin on my leg. I've never appreciated his comfort more as I stroke his fur with one hand and page through the album with the other.

I haven't seen any of these pictures since my mother first brought them home from the pharmacy on Main Street, where she always had them printed. I grit my teeth as I study the first set of photographs taken when I would've been 9 or 10. It's painful to witness the sad little girl posing for the camera with a forced smile edged against her lips. Her brown eyes are vacant and would remain that way until she graduated high school and escaped her personal hell.

I sat on my bed in each picture, hugging an oversized stuffed mouse made with a fuzzy pink material and buttons for eyes. I don't remember receiving it as a gift or anything. I slept with it for many years until one day, when it mysteriously disappeared. I always suspected Diane threw it because she decided I was too old for stuffed animals. Although it was homemade, I don't know where it came from. Diane never sewed anything that I know of.

The colorful quilt covering my bed was always soft when pressed against my skin and retained a hint of my favorite bubble bath's bubblegum scent. Looking at it now, I realize the quilt was also handmade. It was in pristine condition, so probably not old enough to have been Mother's. Since my grandparents died before I was born, maybe it was something she bought from a fundraiser or a church bazaar.

I fail to grasp my mother's need to capture this moment or any other moment. I was homeschooled until the sixth grade, and we didn't go on family vacations. The only friend I had before high school was Rocco. His dad once a picture of us together back them, but Rocco kept it in his room.

Diane was an only child, and my dad was estranged from his two brothers. They never mentioned anyone in their extended families—aunts, uncles, or cousins. I never posed for pictures with either of my parents. I can't recall a photo of the three of us together.

Diane was a devout Baptist, but we didn't go to church. We had our own hour of worship on Sundays, followed by several hours of bible study.

I don't believe I've ever seen a picture of myself at any age younger than the Polaroid from my dad. Where are the photographs from Arizona? Even though my parents were untraditional and the opposite of nurturing, wouldn't *someone* have taken pictures of me as a baby?

I skim through the rest of the photographs, uninterested in witnessing more depressing pictures of myself. Although I suppose at some point I'll have to look through them again if I want to do a thorough job. Determined to find evidence of my life before moving to Iowa, I reach for the oldest-looking album on the shelf. Its rust-colored spine, cracked and crumbling at the edges, features an embossed number too faint to be sure of the date. I can say with certainty it's 1970-something and nothing I've ever seen until now.

The very first photograph takes my breath away. The youngest, most animated versions of my parents I've ever laid eyes on stand on the edge of a pier in an awkward embrace, their broad smiles all but splitting their faces. Diane's engorged stomach makes it difficult for my dad to put his arms all the way around her. They're both as plain-looking as I've always remembered, with average looks that wouldn't get noticed in a crowd.

They're clearly not in Arizona, although they could've been on a road trip or lived somewhere else before I was born. They're each dressed casually in a way that would suggest it's just another day, and they didn't pack for a vacation.

When I remove the photograph from the plastic sleeve to study it closer, another photograph drops into my lap: a picture of a newborn.

I drop the photo of my parents to study the newborn a little closer. The dark-haired baby lays on what appears to be a quilted bed. Bundled in a pink blanket with a pink bow on her head, it's fair to assume the infant is female. Her eyes are closed, and her tiny pink lips are parted either mid-yawn or in a deep sleep.

My heart skips when I notice the small, clover-shaped birthmark above the newborn's right eyelid. It matches the one on the brunette girl in the Polaroid.

I turn the photograph over to see my mother wrote, *"Our sweet Josephine."*

Whiskey churns through my gut.

Who *is* this girl? If she's Josephine, then who the hell am I?

The only person who can give me definitive answers may be dying. Still, there's one other person who could possibly add helpful input.

With the baby picture and Polaroid in hand, I tuck Henry into his kennel and head over to Rocco's house. I'll have to put my complicated feelings for him aside long enough to see if he knows *anything* about the other girl.

No one answers when I knock on the front door. The sound of canned laughter drifts through one of the cracked windows at my side, accompanied by the telling flicker of lights. Deciding he's watching TV, I knock a little harder a second time. The door creaks open.

Swallowing the lump forming in my throat, I take cautious steps inside, prepared to be bombarded with nostalgia. To my surprise, the interior is completely remodeled. The wall separating the kitchen and dining room has been removed and replaced with a walnut beam. Nonna's pink curtains, cracked linoleum, and floral wallpaper are gone. Roman shades, engineered walnut flooring, and a neutral coat of paint create a modern vibe. A quick glance into the kitchen reveals stainless steel appliances, handsome walnut cabinets, and herringbone tiled flooring.

"Rocco?" I call out, heading toward the living room where his grandmother kept the television.

"No!" a man hollers from down the hallway, stopping me dead in my tracks. *"No! I won't let you!"*

It's Rocco. He must be having a nightmare.

After witnessing some horrors throughout my career, I have become familiar with the side effects of PTSD. It's one of the reasons I brought Henry home. Considering the statistics involving veterans who suffer from the same condition, I wouldn't be at all surprised to learn that's what's taking place.

If I wake him, he'll more than likely be embarrassed. Maybe even angry. If I sneak back outside, he'll never know I was here—unless he's installed a security system since moving in. Going with Option B, I spin back to the front door.

I come face-to-face with a skeleton with beady, protruding eyes and snow-white hair.

It reaches for me.

I drop the photos and scream.

CHAPTER 4
PRESENT DAY

Josephine

Once my initial shock subsides and my heart slows to its usual pace, I realize it's most definitely not a zombie standing in my way. It's Rocco's grandmother. The once pudgy woman has become little more than a pile of flesh and bones. The way her dark eyes and broad cheeks have sunken in, I can't exactly blame myself for mistaking her as a creature of the night. Long strands of white hair hang past bony shoulders visible beneath a thin white nightgown several sizes too large.

Eyes stinging with emotion, I all at once remember the way her entire face would light with one of her rare smiles. Although strict, she showed me more love and compassion than my parents combined.

"Nonna," I say, slapping my hand over my chest. "I'm so sorry. You scared me."

"*Tu sei quella ragazza,*" she whispers in a gravelly voice.

I never understood much of what Nonna said as a girl, but I think she's trying to place me since I believe "*tu sei*" roughly translates to "you are." I picked up some Italian from Rocco over time.

"It's me, Nonna," I say with a friendly smile. "It's Josephine."

"Nonna!" Rocco calls out from the hallway. "Nonna, what's wrong?"

"She's okay," I assure him as he enters the room.

Warmth drains from my face when I catch his expression. Veins bulging from his neck, lips snarled, eyes dark as night, he's ready to tear someone apart. With his next shuttering breath, the anger disappears, and he's throwing me a crooked smirk. "Jo?"

Realizing he's wearing nothing more than a pair of boxer briefs, I quickly avert my gaze. In the quick glance I'm afforded of his bare chest, impressively defined with muscle, you'd think I'd plummeted into an active volcano. Heat burns everywhere. *Damn him for still being so attractive.*

He snags a blanket from the back of a leather recliner and spreads it over his grandmother's slender shoulders. I'm aware he's taller than the average man. Still, the way he towers over her like a giant adds to my embarrassment of allowing a frail old woman to frighten me half to death.

"What are you doing here?" he asks me, his sleepy voice muddled with confusion.

"Sorry I woke you. I came over to ask about the Polaroid my dad gave you. The front door was open —I thought maybe you were watching TV. Nonna caught me by surprise."

"She gets a little confused at night," he explains, rubbing a hand across her bony back. "The TV seems to soothe her." He crouches down to her eye level. "Let's get you back in bed, Nonna." After gently steering her toward the hallway, he calls over his shoulder, "There's beer in the fridge. Help yourself."

My hands tremble as I collect the photographs from the floor before heading to the refrigerator and plucking a bottled beer from the glass shelf. Instead of closing the door, I pause to study its contents.

Milk, orange juice, fresh fruits and vegetables, salmon, yogurt, eggs—he's still the same health nut he became in high school while we were dating. He'd put on a little weight when he first hit puberty and was convinced he needed to eat something other than his grandmother's Italian dishes, heavy on sugars and carbs. I smile when remembering how he'd sneak several bites of my mint chocolate malts whenever we went to Hickory Park for barbecue.

"Still hungry?" he calls out behind me with a teasing laugh. "Help yourself to whatever looks good. Grab me a beer, too."

Embarrassed for getting caught snooping, I quickly add another bottle to my grip and turn to him with my chin ducked low. I'm relieved to discover he's thrown on a pair of cotton shorts with the same gray ARMY t-shirt from earlier.

"I was just admiring your continued commitment to healthy food," I tell him. "I'm on the road a lot, so my condo's fridge is usually pretty bare except for a few takeout boxes."

He quirks a brow. "No husband or kids to feed?"

"It's just me and Henry. I don't exactly have time for a family."

"You sound like Papá," he grumbles, swiping

both beer bottles from my hand. "It has nothing to do with your career, Jo. It's about the choices you make." He removes the tops on each bottle and hands one back to me. With a tilt of his head, inviting me to follow, he moves into the living room. "I know a few detectives, and they're all married with kids."

"What about *your* choices?" I challenge with a slight sneer, scurrying to catch up with him. He always assumed he knew what was best for me, and he was usually right. Still, this judgment feels hypocritical, considering he isn't wearing a wedding band. "Although I seriously love what you've done with this place, it's clearly designed to be a bachelor pad. Why haven't *you* settled down?"

"Lacy curtains and ancient flooring weren't going to do well in today's market." He settles into the leather couch facing the matching recliner before taking a long drink of his beer, eyes directed at the ceiling. I'm far too interested in watching his long throat flex with each swallow. Why couldn't he have aged into one of those men with a thin ring of hair and a healthy gut? Lowering the bottle, his gaze rolls back to mine. "I fixed it up so it'll sell when Nonna's gone."

I perch on the other end of the couch and take a

tentative sip of the dark beer, wishing it was whiskey. Maybe then my shoulders would loosen a little. "Is she unwell?"

He lifts one shoulder. "Old age. The day nurse I hired thinks maybe she's developing the start of dementia."

"I'm so sorry, Roc."

"Shit happens. We all die eventually." He tips his beer back for another drink. "I'll gladly take every extra day I'm given."

"What do you do with yourself now that you're retired?"

"I bought a gym down by campus with an old buddy...decided I better find something to keep me busy while I'm here. Remember Chris Anderson?"

"Of course," I answer with a warm smile. "Chris was always a good guy." Once Rocco and I started dating, Chris became a loyal friend of mine as well. Sadness slithers through my belly when I realize I haven't seen Chris in decades.

"He served in the Marine Corps. We figured it's a good way to keep an eye on some of the students... play big brother to those needing some direction."

I flash him another smile from behind my raised bottle. "You have that role down pat." I take a long sip, afraid of whatever nostalgia I'll see reflected in his gaze if I look his way. "What else are you up to? Seeing anyone?"

"There was only one woman I was serious about after you," he offers with a stony expression. "It started up a few months after I moved back. She had a kid from a prior relationship. I grew to love her little girl, but things got complicated, and they moved away."

"That sucks," I say when noticing his tense expression and hunched shoulders.

"It was a long time ago." He gives a minuscule head shake before slugging down the rest of his beer. I wait for him to elaborate more about this ex-girlfriend when he sets the empty bottle on the coffee table. Instead, he asks, "What were you saying about a Polaroid?"

"That's what was inside the envelope my dad asked you to give me." I pass the Polaroid to him. "Do you recognize the brunette girl?"

Squinting at the photograph in his hands, he shakes his head. "I don't think so."

"Do you ever remember seeing me with blond hair when we were young?"

"The first time I met you." He nods with certainty before catching my perplexed expression. "You don't remember being a blonde back then?"

"No. I was always—" I stop with a gasp when something occurs to me. "Oh my god. The cleansing shampoo!"

Rocco's brows scrunch together. "What?"

"Diane used to wash my hair every couple of months with something she called a 'cleansing shampoo.' She said it stripped the filth from my hair. I thought it was weird because I never actually *got dirty,* but never questioned it. It smelled funny and darkened the sink when she rinsed my hair. I'm just realizing now that smell was ammonia. It's what they put in hair dye to open hair cuticles."

"Why would your mom dye your hair when you were young?"

I tilt my head. "Seriously? I think we're beyond questioning my parents' actions."

"Good point."

I gesture to the photo. "Turn it around."

"*I'm sorry?*" he reads aloud before holding the photograph away. "What's that about?"

"Your guess is as good as mine." I hand him the newborn photograph. "This was in an album I've never seen before, stuck behind a picture of my parents when Diane was pregnant. I should add that I've never seen a picture of myself before the age of seven or eight until this Polaroid, and I'm almost positive that baby isn't me."

"How do you know?"

"The birthmark above her right eye. The brown-haired girl in the Polaroid has the exact same one."

He glances away from the picture to throw me a friendly grin. "That's fast work, detective. Who do you think she is?"

"Turn it over." I tip my beer back, guzzling what's left as he reads Diane's inscription.

"What the hell *is* this?" Rocco demands. "What do you think your dad was trying to apologize for?"

"At first, I thought maybe he had an affair, and that girl was my sister." I take the photographs from him, studying the two little girls with a shake of my head. They may as well both be complete strangers. "Now I don't know what to believe."

Grumbling something under his breath, Rocco takes my empty bottle and sets it next to his. I'm ready to ask what he's doing until he scoots in closer and grips my knees in his hands, shocking me to my core. Familiarity overwhelms me, rattling my last shred of confidence. Why does he still have this effect on me?

"We've always suspected your parents were hiding a pretty big secret, Jo. It drove Papá insane when he couldn't find a bulletproof way to help you. Nonna, too. She didn't like your parents the minute you arrived." I despise the sympathetic look he's projecting when he continues. "I can't tell you how many times I talked Papá out of calling social services. Now that I'm older and wiser, I realize they probably wouldn't have given his reports the time of day anyway. Aside from the fact that your parents wouldn't let you leave the house the first few years after you moved here, what could he have done to prove something wasn't right?"

"He could've demanded they ask for a DNA test from my parents," I huff humorlessly. "Hiding me from the public eye for all those years, secretly dyeing my hair, failing to produce any evidence of my life before we moved here...it all points to one thing, Roc." Tears prick my eyes when I confess the truth. "I think I was kidnapped."

His gaze doesn't waver from mine as he gives a despondent nod. "What are you going to do about it?"

"I'm going to start by searching for my birth family," I decide. "Then I'm going to find out what happened to the real Josephine." To my dismay, a set of tears race down my cheeks. "God, this sucks." Swiping my arm over my face, I laugh and look away.

"Wouldn't it be a kick in the ass to discover my real parents were a normal, fun-loving couple who planned to spoil me with trips to the beach and Disney World?"

"The chances of that are probably slim." Rocco takes my chin between his thumb and pointer finger. "Look at me, Jo."

With my last bit of energy, I grip his forearm as my eyes slide back to meet his.

"I'm here for you. As little or as much as you need me. Until you tell me to leave, I'm not going anywhere." Sliding his other hand against my face, he strokes his warm thumb along my jaw. "I gave up on relationships a long time ago, but I haven't given up on you. Take whatever it is you want or need from me, Jo."

Our close proximity and his intimate expression, on top of the recent revelations about my childhood, are all too damn much. Caving like a house of cards, I lean into him, needing to feel the assuring strength of his lips.

His gaze frantically searches mine. "You sure about this?" he rasps, his breath scorching hot against my mouth. "Once we start something, there's no guarantee I can simply walk away, even when you decide you're done with me."

"Would you shut up and kiss me already?" Deep down, I acknowledge what he's saying and understand I could be making a massive mistake by giving in to my needs. But logic is nowhere to be seen when I thread my fingers inside his hair and drag his mouth down to mine.

CHAPTER 5
BEFORE

Rocco

After the new neighbors move in, I don't see the little girl for weeks. Then one day, I have a feeling she's in the backyard because I hear the thud of a rubber ball hitting the fence over and over. It's the weekend, and the man left in their station wagon a few hours ago. The woman must be somewhere inside.

I race over the hole in the fence to watch her. This time, her hair is brown instead of yellow, and dark shadows linger beneath her eyes. She looks pretty mad the way she's chucking the red ball at the fence. She's even smaller than I remember, or maybe it's just because the sundress she's wearing is several sizes too large.

"Hi!" I call out to her. "Remember me?"

Her brown eyes dart to the house before she shuffles over to me in the grass. "Roc-o?" she whispers, her voice light and airy like a cartoon character.

"That's right," I say, flashing my biggest smile. "What's your name?"

Her eyes slide back to the house again before she answers in a tiny voice, "J-Josep'ine."

I know it kinda makes me a bully, but I laugh. It sounds like a really big name for such a little girl. "How about I call you 'Jo' instead?"

With a shy smile, she dips her chin twice.

"Do you want to come over to play, Jo? We can kick your ball around the yard or whatever you want."

Looking down at her bare feet, she gives me a little shake of her head. "I can't."

"Even if you ask?"

"They won't let me."

I remember my conversation with the people I thought to be parents and suddenly feel mad for her. "The man and the lady you're living with?"

She nods.

"Who are they?"

She glances down, wiggling her toes in the grass. "Mommy and Daddy."

Huh, I think. *That's weird. What is going on with these people?*

Since she's really young and doesn't seem comfortable with me, I decide not to push her any more about who those people really might be to her. I'm just glad she's finally talking to me. "How old are you?"

Still looking down, she tugs at one of the straps on her sundress. "Ummm...six."

"Six?" I repeat, my eyes growing wide. "So you're in kindergarten?"

She gives me another little shake of her head before looking up at me. "I don't go to school. Mommy teaches me here."

"That sucks," I say. Even though I hate school, I would hate it more if I was stuck at home all day and unable to play with my friends at recess. Now I understand why she looks so lonely. The man and woman must be even meaner than I thought. "Where did you live before you moved here?"

"At my house, with my mommy."

I let out a little laugh. I get that a six-year-old

might not be too good with geography, but wouldn't she at least know the name of the town? "Did you live far away?"

She shrugs. "Don't know."

While she bends to pick a dandelion near her feet, I cross my arms. How can she be six? Maybe she's slow. I guess I could try to help her out. Our class was once paired with a kindergarten class at school and we had to play a bunch of games that were supposed to help them learn how to count and stuff. If she's going to be home every day, I may as well teach her something useful.

"We could play a game through the fence," I tell her. "It won't be easy, but we'll figure it out somehow. Would you like that, Jo?"

Her cheeks lift and turn pink with the biggest smile in the world. What a cutie.

I'm starting to feel really sorry for this kid.

———

Papá is home. For good this time.

It happened so suddenly that sometimes I have a hard time believing it's true. Nonna says his heart isn't working right, and the Army decided they didn't want him anymore because of it, so he flew back to live with us. He's been kinda grumpy since he returned, but having him around has still made me the happiest I've ever been.

I peek inside his bedroom first thing every morning to make sure he's still there and his return wasn't just some dream I had. He slept a lot at first. Nonna said the time change from Germany and the long flight wore him out.

Then, after a few days, he started getting up in time for breakfast. Afterward, he'd work on little things around the house that needed fixing, like the squeaky back door and the leaky kitchen faucet. Since school is out for the summer, I've been getting up each day in time to watch him get ready. He sometimes lets me help with his projects. Other times, he gets kinda crabby and tells me to play outside because he needs time alone.

I've been playing with Jo every afternoon since the day she told me her name. We try to be quiet because she doesn't think her parents want me to play with her. She's a smart kid, and I love finding ways to make her laugh. Whenever I hear her high-pitched little giggle, I can't stop smiling. Every time I head over to the fence, I find her waiting for me on the other side.

I'm worried about her. Does she just sit outside all day long? What will she do once it starts getting cold in the fall? Why won't her parents let her come to my house? Why don't they ever take her anywhere?

"We have new neighbors," I tell Papá one morning as he's shaving over the bathroom sink. "It's a mom and a dad with a little girl named Jo. She told me she's six, but she's really small and acts more like a super little kid. Her mom teaches her school at home. I don't think they take her anywhere. *Ever.* She acts really lonely, so I've started hanging out with her. She's pretty smart and catches on fast. We have to play different games through the hole in the fence because her parents won't let her come over."

Papá's dark eyes meet mine in the mirror, making me shiver. Now that I'm older, it's easy to tell I'm his kid. We have the same nose and mouth, the same thick black hair. Except he's way taller with a lot of muscles, and he knows how to look super scary when he wants, something Nonna said helped when he was in charge of soldiers in the Army. No one's ever scared of me since I'm built like a string bean.

"Why won't they let her come over?" he asks, sounding mad.

I lift both shoulders and puff out a big breath. "I dunno. They seem kinda mean. I don't think her mom likes her very much."

He cleans the shaving cream off his razor in the water-filled sink. "I'll go over there and introduce myself." He continues shaving his face. "I'll straighten things out."

———

That night after dinner, I swear Papá is at the new neighbors' *forever* before he finally returns home. His face is blotched with red spots when he stomps through the kitchen. He doesn't say anything when he heads straight to the freezer for the container of strawberry gelato Nonna brought home earlier in the day.

With her hands on her hips, Nonna scowls at him when she asks in Italian, "What is this about? Why do you look that way?"

"That man and woman next door are filthy liars," Papá answers, also in Italian. He gives me a worried glance before he grabs three bowls out of the cupboard and begins scooping gelato into each one. "I don't want my son going over there anymore."

"I can speak Italian, too, you know," I tell him with a huff. "What did they lie about?"

"They said they don't want you near their daughter because you're a bad influence. They told me you bullied her and claimed you hit her."

Anger burns my face. "But I didn't—"

"Hush, boy!" he snaps, tossing a spoon into Nonna's dish and handing it to her. "I know you're not a bully, and you would never raise your hand to a woman. That's why I say they're liars. I think you're right about the girl's age, too. I could see her in the next room. She was curled around herself in a little ball. She looked terrified."

"Why would they lie about her age?"

"I'm not sure. But I want you to stay far away from them. We don't need a reason for them to invent more excuses and accuse you of something else you didn't do. If they ever claimed something untrue to the authorities, your future would be over. I want you to stay far away from the girl, too."

"But, Papá—"

"There'll be no buts about it, Rocco! You can tell a lot about a man by how he treats his child. That mother, too. Their daughter must've been an unplanned pregnancy. Maybe their religion prevented the mother from getting an abortion. They're not good people. That girl would be better off with a different family."

"What about us? Could she come stay here?"

"That's not an option, Rocco." Papá's jaw tightens. "Besides, they would never allow such a thing. They clearly don't want us meddling in their business."

"Can't we tell someone, like the principal at my school? They're always telling us if something isn't right at home—"

"I don't want you getting involved!" Papá roars. "This discussion is over!"

With a firm look that stops me from saying anything more, he takes his bowl of gelato and goes into the living room, leaving me alone with Nonna. When I hear the hum of the TV, I shuffle closer to her.

"The girl is lonely," I whisper in Italian. "Just like you said." I blink away the tears starting to form. They're due to frustration more than anything. Whatever's going on next door isn't right. I don't like how they're treating Jo. "I think she's scared of her parents, too. If I don't go over there, she'll be left alone with those people."

"You're a good boy." Nonna sets her bowl of

gelato back on the countertop. She then pulls me into a tight hug and kisses the top of my head. "This will not be the end of your friendship with her. I will make sure of it. Your papá will understand with time."

CHAPTER 6
PRESENT DAY

Josephine

jerk awake to shouting and the weight of an arm flinging over my side. Disoriented, I blink rapidly against darkness.

"Stop!" Rocco yells from right behind me. *"Don't make me hurt you!"*

I gently shrug him off me and sit upright as my vision adjusts to Rocco's naked silhouette on the bed beside me. Details from earlier return with the force of a mallet striking a gong. Once he kissed me like I asked, neither of us could stop what came next.

The sex was fantastic, and it felt terrific to lose

myself in the luxury of pleasure, but still. I must keep a clear head if I'm going to uncover my true identity and the reason my parents abducted me.

Wincing, I carefully swing my legs over the side of the queen bed and begin collecting my articles of clothing scattered across the bedroom floor. I can't believe I allowed my emotions to dictate my actions. It's so unlike me. Then again, I'm not myself around Rocco. I seem to lose all sense of responsibility when faced with his tantalizingly fit body and beautiful smile. I can't afford to fall victim to his kindness like I did when we were teenagers.

I turn away from him, pulling on my undergarments with the stealth of a ninja. I made a grave mistake when coming over to show him the photographs. The empathy he exhibited reminded me all too well of the younger version of him who had loved me unconditionally. If I don't run from him and the situation now, it might be too late to fight against the feelings I buried all those years ago.

I'm slipping my sweatshirt over my head when a deliciously dark chuckle fills the room. "I'm surprised you stayed this long," Rocco muses.

Keeping my back turned to him, I step into my joggers. "It's nothing personal. I need to let Henry out."

"Bring him over. It's early, and I'm not finished with you."

The possessiveness in his deep timbre warms me down to my toes. I forgot what it's like to be involved with an alpha male, probably because Rocco was the only one of that type to make my list of suitors. I'd be tempted to stay for another round if my life wasn't so convoluted.

"Easy, tiger," I say with a soft laugh that stems more from nerves than humor. I turn to face him with a dismissive smile. "This was fun, but I have more important things to do while I'm back."

"I'll help you dig into this mess with your parents," he offers, sitting up and brushing his hair out of his eyes. "I told you I'm here for you—I can clear my calendar with a phone call to Chris and Nonna's nurse."

"Let's not make this any more complicated than it needs to be. I'll probably head home in another day or two." I jerk my gaze away from the temptation of his beautiful body and start for the bedroom door. "I promise to say goodbye before I leave."

His bare feet land on the floor with a *thud* before his warm fingers wrap around my wrist. "I warned you, Jo." He nudges me around to face him. "Just because you decide you've had enough fun with me and don't need anything else doesn't mean I'll simply walk away. Our bond as kids is still there— maybe stronger than ever after our conversation last night." His eyes sweep over my face before his voice deepens. "My feelings for you...they didn't fade with time."

Something dislodges inside my chest and rises in my throat.

It would be far too easy to love this man again. Then again, I'm not certain I stopped loving him after the first round.

"I don't have time for this," I snap, prying his grip off my arm and spinning around to open the door. "I appreciate your friendship, and that's all this will ever be." I regret glancing back at him when I catch the glare of disappointment burning through his gaze. "Trust me, it's better for both of us this way."

After taking Henry for a 3-mile walk and grabbing breakfast from a little cafe a block from campus called Stomping Grounds, I head back to my parents' house. I finish browsing through the old album where I'd found the photograph of the actual baby

Josephine. Hoping to find another clue, I pull out every photograph to search for more hidden messages or secret photos. Aside from more pictures of a pregnant Diane and some younger pictures of my parents with a bunch of strangers, the effort ends up being a waste of time.

Shortly before the noon hour, I take the dreaded drive to the nursing home. Although it will be difficult to face my incapacitated dad without wanting to shake answers out of him, the trip seems unavoidable at this point.

I don't know what I was expecting, but discovering my dad sitting upright and fully clothed in an armchair comes as a complete shock. When the middle-aged nurse leaves me alone with him in the small room, I have to bite my tongue and remind myself of everything the nurse said—he can function to a small degree, like chewing and swallowing when he's fed, but he isn't all there.

Although he's only 73, he's aged considerably since my last visit to Iowa and could pass for someone in their late eighties. I'd estimate he's lost at least 40 pounds, and he didn't weigh much to begin with. His skin was always a little crepey from spending countless hours tending to the yard, but his dark veins weren't as prevalent before. Deep lines crease his pale face, and his eyelids droop, significantly altering his appearance. I don't know that I would've recognized him in passing.

Mustering the slightest amount of enthusiasm proves impossible. Seeing him only reminds me of the dark childhood they created for me and ignites my growing desire for answers.

"Hi, Dad." My voice is dull, and my lips remain tight as I approach him. His green eyes track me without the slightest spark of recognition. I sit on the edge of the bed, mere feet from where he's sitting, and study his expression when I blurt, "Rocco gave me the Polaroid."

Nothing.

"Call me crazy, but I'm starting to think you and my mother were hiding me from the world when I was a kid because you abducted me."

His blank gaze fixated on me sends a cold shiver down my spine. What other kind of unimaginable things has he done in his lifetime?

"Why, Dad?" I ask, clenching my teeth when tears sting the back of my eyes. "Who were my real parents? Why did you take me from them? Why did you two spend my entire childhood acting like you hated me for existing? What happened to the real Josephine?"

My dad's lips twitch, then gape. I hold my breath while awaiting his response, grateful for the temporary relief from the greasy nursing home odor clogging my sinuses.

"Excuse me," a young man interrupts from the doorway.

Swiping my wrist over my damp eyes, I turn to him. "What do you need?" I demand, embarrassed to be interrupted when I'm most vulnerable.

The male nurse, likely 19 or 20, appears unfazed by my curt reply when he smiles. "The nurse's station received a call from someone inquiring about your father's status. We thought you'd like to speak with them since you're here."

Laughter sticks to my throat. Other than Rocco, who's tethered to my dad's lawn, who would care enough to check in? A bill collector? "Who is it?"

"He says he's Frank's father, so I suppose that would make him your grandfather."

I release a sharp cackle. "Impossible. His dad died before I was born."

The nurse's gaze flickers down the hallway as he shifts his weight and tugs at the neckline of his blue scrubs. "Umm, I don't know what to say. That's what I was told."

"Let me speak to him," I decide with an impatient sigh.

The nurse enters the room and lifts the corded phone's receiver on the nightstand beside the bed. After punching a few buttons, he hands the receiver to me before slipping back into the hallway.

"May I ask who's calling?" I say into the receiver.

"This is Roger Kelly," a reedy voice answers. "Frank is my son. Who's this?"

My gut sloshes with unease. The man sounds quite elderly. What reason would he have to lie about being family? It's not like my parents had a large estate that would garner attention from scammers. Then again, who knows what else they may have lied about?

"I'm a friend of the family," I tell him.

"A what?" he yells back.

"A family friend," I repeat in a much louder voice. "Where are you calling from, Mr. Kelly?"

"Sunshine Manor in Baltimore. But don't let the name fool you—it's not so sunny today."

"How long have you lived there?"

"In this place? A couple'a decades by now, I suppose." He lets out a friendly chuckle. "But I've lived in Baltimore for *ninety-four* years, if you can believe it. My entire life. I was born during the Great Depression, grew up in Federal Hill. I was in the Korean War for a year before I returned home to marry my high school sweetheart. We raised our three boys in a row house just down the street from where I grew up. After my wife passed away, I was forced to move here. It was too much to keep up on my own. Those steep stairs didn't do me any favors, either."

For once, I'm happy to let an elderly person ramble on. My parents never spoke of my grandparents, so this information, if it's to be believed, is all new to me. The only reason I was aware my dad had brothers was because I took a call from one of them shortly after Diane had died. He said he had gone to a lot of trouble to track my parents down and simply wanted to know the details of his sister-in-law's funeral arrangements. My dad had taken the phone away before I could get more information from my alleged uncle.

"When did you last see Frank?"

"Oh, that was a long, *long* time ago. He and Diane only returned a few times after they moved out of Baltimore. They never brought my granddaughter back to see me or her uncles after they left here. They always had some kind of outlandish excuse.

Claimed flying from Washington to Maryland was too much for a girl her age."

"Washington?" I choke out. "As in the state?"

"That's where they told us they went, but my oldest boy later learned they were in Iowa after Diane died. They wouldn't even let us speak with my granddaughter on the telephone. She was a precious little thing. I haven't seen her since she was a little peanut—maybe five or six years old. Back then, they invited me and my other sons' families over every Sunday night for dinner since we all lived in the same neighborhood."

Baltimore is a helluva long way from Arizona, I think, while glaring at the feeble man who pretended for decades to be my birth father. Since the nurse came into the room, his mouth has remained shut. Whether or not he'd been attempting to speak earlier, a hint of something in his gaze makes me wonder if he's comprehending my side of the conversation.

"When Diane and Frank left with my sweet Josephine, it gutted me. I prayed forever that they'd let me see her again. After a while, I made peace with the fact that it'd never happen, so I started begging Diane to at least send me pictures. She finally gave in when Jo was a little older. Poor thing never looked too happy." His voice cracks with emotion when he says, "From that point on, I began to pray that she was alright."

Even if the man on the telephone isn't my biological grandfather, I can't help feeling sorry for him. It's one of the few revelations I've learned in the past 24 hours that makes sense, considering the kind of people who raised me.

"I have reason to believe Diane and Frank didn't let you see your granddaughter because they were hiding something significant from you and the rest of your family," I tell him.

"I suspect that may have been the case as well."

Excitement rushes through my body. *What does he know?* Rehashing everything I've learned over the telephone feels unusually cruel. Someone Roger's age might not survive the shock. I grab my phone and open my favorite travel app. "If I came to Baltimore, would you mind if I stopped by for a visit?"

CHAPTER 7
BEFORE

Rocco

Jo's parents think they've "trained" her well enough that she will stay home when told.

Now that she's turned eleven, they leave her home alone all the time. Like, a lot. Whenever I see her mom's car leave their driveway, I head back to the hole in the fence and wait for Jo to tell me how long she thinks her mom will be gone. If it's more than a half hour, Jo lets me in through her front door, or she comes over to my house. Ever since her mom took a part-time job at the University's cafeteria, there are days when she's gone for five or more hours at a time. On those summer days, Jo and I like to go somewhere fun. She loves to ride on the front of my ten-speed bike when we decide to head somewhere far away.

Whenever we hang out at places like Hickory Park for ice cream or Great Plains for pizza (Jo's favorite), we tell people we're brother and sister. No one really knows me in town unless they recognize me from busing tables at Bella's, Tita's restaurant, which doesn't happen often. Sometimes, we grab lunch at Bella's when Nonna cooks, and she'll make us a free meal.

Since Papá started managing the sporting goods store, he has no idea what I'm doing all day and doesn't seem to care. Nonna has grown to love Jo enough that my secret is safe with her. But Papá's become strict in the past couple of years, so I have to finish my chores before I take Jo anywhere. If I either forget or don't do something the way he expects, I get a major ass-chewing when he comes home. He loves to tell me I'm "a pussy" and lets me know the military wouldn't take me if I applied.

When hanging out with Jo away from home, I sometimes forget all about our stressful situations at home. It feels like we're normal kids, especially when my friend Chris comes along. He's cool with Jo even though she's two years younger than us, so I've started inviting him along more often. Sometimes Chris calls us "The Three Amigos" because he's really into that movie with Steve Martin, Chevy Chase, and Martin Short.

I dream of the day we can take Jo to see a movie at The Ranch drive-in theater. She's never seen a movie besides the ones that sometimes air on basic cable. I wish her mom would take a night job so we could somehow make it happen.

One afternoon in mid-August, when it's like, 110 degrees out, I give Jo a ride on my bike to meet Chris at Hickory Park for ice cream. Jo always orders the mint chocolate malt, and I get the banana split. I swear Chris never orders the same thing twice. Working for Tita has been great because I can afford to spoil Jo when we're together.

"Guess what?" Jo asks us, a mustache of mint ice cream smeared across her upper lip. "Diane says I get to go to middle school next year."

"Who's Diane?" Chris asks.

"Her mom," I say before grinning at Jo. "For real?"

Wiping her bare arm over her mouth, she nods excitedly. "She says I'm finally caught up to other kids my age."

With my mouth hanging open, I drop my spoon. I can't believe they're finally going to let her leave the house. At least without having to sneak out. "Jo, that's awesome! You'll get to go to school with us!" When I remember Chris and I only have one year left at the middle school, I roll my shoulders forward. "I mean, for a little while, anyway."

The way Jo's bright smile rounds her cheeks, she looks even younger than usual. "She said I get to ride the bus and everything."

"Middle school girls can be really mean," Chris tells her with a mouthful of his butterscotch and chocolate malt. "You're probably better off staying at home."

While he's busy digging his spoon around in his ice cream, Jo and I exchange a look. Chris doesn't know the whole story about Jo. He doesn't know she'd never been to a single restaurant or store in town until this summer. Her parents only let her leave to visit the doctor and dentist. I have to give her credit for how cool she's been about everything. I'm the only one who notices how she secretly gets excited about our adventures.

"We can keep an eye on her," I tell Chris. "We won't let anyone pick on her. Besides, she's cooler than most girls. I bet the mean girls will leave her alone."

"You think so?" Jo asks, sitting a little taller.

"I'll make sure of it," I promise.

I suddenly feel a strong need to protect her from everything she's about to experience for the first time. There's so much she won't understand about the way middle school works. If a girl has ever bullied her, she probably wouldn't have remembered.

I only have a couple of weeks to make sure she's ready.

———

A couple of days later, Nonna decides it's time to take me shopping for new school supplies and clothes since I grew a few inches after finishing 7th grade and my jeans have become embarrassingly short. Jo doesn't understand this tradition and says her mom bought everything she'll need. I cringe at the news, wondering what kind of things her weirdo mom has picked out. Jo could get teased if she shows up for school with the wrong type of folders and stuff. Worse yet, I have a terrible feeling everything Jo wears is from a second-hand store. That alone will make her an easy target for older girls.

When I tell Nonna my worries, she explains that Papá has sent along a set amount for everything I'll need. She tells me I can spend the money however I'd like, and she won't tell if I spend some of it on Jo.

"Wait and see how it goes," she says on the bus ride to the North Grand Mall. "You could bring her other things for her to wear when she gets on the bus. You will soon be a waiter at Bella's and have more money of your own."

With that plan in place, I use most of the money from Papá for the things I need and $30 on a pink sweater I see on a high school girl working at The Limited. I figure I can throw it in my backpack on the first day of school, just in case.

Before long, the days and nights become way cooler with the arrival of September. I'm way more worried than Jo on the first day of school, scared I've forgotten to prepare her for something important. She doesn't seem at all fazed when I find her waiting on the curb outside of their house that morning. With her curly dark hair left down around her shoulders, acid-washed jeans, sneakers, and a long-sleeved t-shirt, she doesn't look too bad. At least I don't think there's anything unusual that will get her noticed. I'm surprised to see her mom even bought her a decent backpack that doesn't look used.

Since her parents don't know we've become friends—or at least I don't *think* they know—I wait in front of my house until the bus arrives. By the time I move in front of her to climb the bus steps, I can feel the excitement vibrating from her. That and I think she's shivering from the morning chill.

"Don't you have a coat?" I ask over my shoulder.

She replies with a wordless shrug. I choose an open bench in the middle and slide over to the window to make room for Jo. Even though I warned her not to stare at anyone, I can tell she's eager to take a good at the other kids sitting around us. She's unusually stiff when she sits next to me, and I can tell she's constantly glancing out the corners of her eyes.

"Relax," I whisper to her, unzipping my backpack. "You're doing great. I have a present for you."

"For real?" She sounds just like me. I probably ask her that ten times every day.

"Just…don't freak out."

I hand her the bag with the pink sweater inside. When she pulls it out and unfolds it, her lips shake, and she blinks her eyes like a hundred times.

"Don't cry," I whisper. "Be cool."

"But the tag is still on it," she whispers. "I've never owned anything brand-new."

"I saw an older girl wearing it at the mall, figured it'd look good on you, too. Plus, it'll keep you warm."

"No one has ever been as nice to me as you, Roc." She quickly wipes a hand over her eyes before leaning in to kiss my cheek. "Thank you."

My face burns when she backs away. I'm too flustered to speak.

As she slips on the sweater and throws me one of her biggest smiles, I vow I'll do anything to protect her.

———

The eighth graders have a different recess period than sixth graders, but there are a handful of minutes when the two overlap. Chris and I run outside when the bell rings, eager to find Jo and ask her how her day has gone so far.

"Start that way, and I'll meet you back here," I tell him, pointing to the far end of the yard where students stand around in small groups. I weave through the kids nearby, not looking at any faces. Jo's sweater should be bright enough that she'll be easy to find. A few minutes pass before Chris and I meet in the middle.

"You didn't see her either?" I ask with a heavy feeling in my gut.

Chris shrugs. "Maybe she didn't come outside."

"The monitor doesn't let anyone inside."

"Unless they have to use the bathroom," he reminds me.

I search the yard for one of the teachers watching over us. Once I find her, I ask if I can run inside to use the bathroom. She looks annoyed but gives me permission.

I sprint inside, stopping at the nearest girl's bathroom and calling Jo's name through the doorway. "It's me, Roc," I add.

There's a sniffle, then, "What do you want?" Her voice is impatient and thick.

"Why aren't you outside? Is everything okay?"

"Don't come in here!" she cries.

Screw that, I decide as I enter the room. She's clearly upset.

"Where are you?" I demand, bending to look beneath the dozen sets of stalls. I spot her sneakers in one and head over to knock on it. "What's wrong? Why are you in here?" I pause, waiting for her to open the door. "Come on, open up. I'll crawl under the door if I have to."

Finally, I hear the latch swivel and the door opens

a crack. "Don't be mad," she begs. "After they ruined it, I waited until I got in here to cry."

The muscles in my stomach harden. "What's ruined?"

"The sweater you bought me." She releases a tight whine before bursting into tears. "I'm so sorry, Roc! I tried acting cool like you said, but they called me a baby and said I'd never fit in! One of them had a scissors and—"

A growl rips through my throat when I push on the door and find her huddled in the corner, the ruined sweater clutched inside her hands. It's been cut to shreds.

"Who did it?" I demand, trying to keep my cool. I don't want her to think I'm mad at her. I also don't know how I'll stop myself from totally blowing up and going crazy on the jerk responsible. It's a weird sensation—one I've never felt until now.

She shakes her head. "I don't want to tell you. He was really mean. He'll just be mean to you, too."

"Let me worry about that." I enter the stall to put my arm around her. "What's his name, Jo?"

Tears drip down to her sneakers when she lowers her chin. "One of the girls told him to stop...she called him Marcus. I think he's a seventh grader."

I know exactly who she's talking about. Marcus

Tanner is a total clown. He's always doing something stupid to get attention. "Don't worry about the sweater…it wasn't that expensive," I say, grabbing a wad of toilet paper and handing it to her. "Wash your face with cold water and wait a minute to leave. Don't let anyone see you upset. Especially not Marcus. You're way stronger than other girls at this school. Hold your ground and let them know you can't be messed with. If he messes with you again, punch him like I taught you to get the message across."

As soon as she starts drying her face, I leave her to search for Marcus.

CHAPTER 8
PRESENT DAY

Josephine

With a flight booked to Baltimore/Washington International Airport, I reluctantly head back to Rocco's house. Before I lift my hand to knock, the door swings open and he appears with a smug grin. It's a little easier to resist his charm when he's fully dressed. In a pair of running shorts and a tank top advertising "Gym 22"—what I assume to be the gym he co-owns—paired with the perspiration dotting his forehead and glistening down his neck, it seems I've interrupted his workout.

"I figured you couldn't stay away for very long,"

he teases, flashing blindly white teeth behind a wide smile.

My eyes roll to the cloudless sky above us. "I need to ask for a favor."

His cocky expression evaporates. "Don't tell me you're already leaving."

"I have to travel out of town for a day or two. I was hoping you could keep an eye on Henry until I return. He can stay at my dad's if you and Nonna don't want him underfoot. He's house-trained and prefers the comfort of his kennel at night if he can't be in a bed. I'd be grateful if you could take him for a walk or two and throw the ball around the yard like last night."

His dark brown eyes harden with suspicion. "Where are you going?"

"Baltimore. While I was visiting my dad this afternoon, my paternal grandfather called. It turns out he's *not* dead, and my parents are *not* from Arizona. I'm going to visit him to see what else he may know that my so-called *parents* neglected to tell me. I hope to track down my dad's two brothers, too."

"That's a lot to process." With a thoughtful expression, he rubs his hand over his chest. "When does your flight leave?"

"In four and a half hours. I figured I'd speak with you about Henry first to ensure I don't have to look into other arrangements before I start re-packing."

"That gives me plenty of time to make a few calls, pack a bag, and shower."

With a cackling laugh, I give a firm shake of my head. "You're *not* coming with me, Roc."

One of his eyebrows lifts. "Give me one good reason."

"Henry. Nonna. Your gym." I tick off the reasons with one hand raised between us, scowling when I release the fourth finger. "And I'm a private person. I need to do this alone."

He mocks me with a countdown of *his* fingers. "Number one, Chris and his wife adore dogs, and their black lab would love to help Henry run off some of that energy. Two, Nonna's in-home nurse has stayed overnight at least a dozen times by now. As for the gym, I'm not scheduled to cover another shift until next week."

Dropping his hand, his expression softens. "As for the fourth thing, I honestly don't care what kind of excuse you come up with because I saw how much this affected you last night when you considered the kidnapping angle. I know you, Jo. Since you're not involved with anyone, I'm willing to bet I know you better than anyone else. If you're going to be stubborn and pretend you don't want more of what went on last night, I'll get a separate room. If you want to be an adult and accept whatever's happening between us, you can use me to blow off a little steam at night." Mischief sparks his eyes when he adds, "In any manner you deem fit. Either way, I'm coming along because I know this shit is eating you up inside, and I don't want you dealing with it on your own when your parents' other lies surface."

I glower back at him while gnashing my teeth together. Based on the resolved look he's giving me, I suspect he won't budge, no matter how much I protest.

And he thinks I'm *stubborn.*

A youthful smile cracks his lips when he realizes I won't put up a fight. "I'll come over as soon as I'm ready. We'll drop Henry at the gym on the way to the airport." He bends down to steal a slow, toe-curling kiss, then he runs back inside. I stare at the open doorway, berating myself for not objecting to his plan.

You're not a pushover. Quit acting like one.

Before I can devise an alternative plan for Henry, Nonna wanders into view. Beneath the sunlight, she isn't as nefarious-looking as she was in the middle of the night. She's wearing a blouse beneath a long dress, and her hair is brushed back into a low braid. My heart skips a little when I assume Rocco had to have been the one to style her hair. I doubt many men would take on caring for their elderly grandmother the way he has.

"Tu sei quella ragazza," she says with a widening of her eyes. It's the same thing she'd said to me the night before, only this time, there's a hint of a smile tugging at her cracked lips. While she may have been suffering from sundowner's before, she appears more cogent in the daylight.

"I'm Josephine from next door," I say to her. My smile fades. "Or maybe not. At this point, who knows my real name?"

"È sepolto nel giardino," Nonna whispers, glancing over her shoulder before clamping a bony hand over my wrist. She repeats the phrase with urgency, then adds, *"Sotto le rose."* Her grip becomes painfully tight.

With my heart hammering, I commit her Italian words to memory, intending to search for a translation. Why does she seem afraid? Is it the disease messing with her head? I pry her fingers from my wrist and pat her arm.

"Why don't we get you settled in front of the TV?" I suggest, leading her back into the living room. Once she's sitting in the recliner beneath a blanket with a rerun of a game show playing, I consider waiting for Rocco to finish his shower so I can get his take on Nonna's ramblings. When I hear his deep voice rumbling in conversation, I head back over to let Henry run outside until it's time to leave.

The second I'm outside, I retrieve my phone from my back jeans pocket and open the language translator app purchased by my station for everyone in the department. It takes a few tries before the app understands my crude Italian.

"You're that girl," is most likely the first thing she said to me, followed by something about "it" being *"buried in the garden"* and *"beneath the roses."*

Crippling chills dribble down my back. I only remember Nonna planting herbs in their backyard. As I enter my dad's driveway, I scan Nonna's backyard to confirm it's rose-free. How would she know about something in my parents' yard? What does she think is buried there? While it could easily be the ramblings of a woman whose mind is fading, nothing seems too far-fetched. I'm not going to ignore a potential lead.

After grabbing a spade and gloves from the garage, I let Henry join me in the backyard. I'd be a terrible liar if I claimed the mere idea of destroying my dad's beloved rose bush didn't fill me with immense pleasure. Even if I were to come up empty-handed, the action of ruining one of the few things he placed on a pedestal instead of his only child could be therapeutic. I was around ten or eleven when he planted it. At the time, he had just started working for a landscaper and was proud of the skills he'd acquired.

The first stab at the roots of the thriving bush, overflowing with symmetrical pink blossoms, proves to be more satisfying than spending an afternoon at the shooting range. Luckily, Ames has avoided freezing temperatures so far, and the dark soil gives way with ease. I destroy the beautiful plant entirely before continuing to dig deeper. Henry joins in on the fun, digging alongside me with the finesse of a crackhead in need of a fix.

Before long, however, the joy of the act is all at once replaced with a nagging fear. *What am I about to find?* My arms turn to rubber as cold sweat springs across my face. What if they buried the *real* Josephine in the same yard I spent my childhood locked inside?

Around the time I convince myself to call the local PD and get their forensics involved, the tip of the spade slams into something metal. *Too late for that call.*

I'm trembling as I toss the spade aside and lower to my knees. With a gloved hand, I clear the dirt away and let out a surprised gasp when the object is fully unearthed.

It's a metal lunchbox featuring Holly Hobbie, a cartoon character wearing a quilted dress and a large bonnet. Holly was beloved by girls at the height of my childhood. Although I didn't have much for toys, I remember wearing an oversized t-shirt featuring the sweet character. I didn't know anything about Holly then, but I sometimes pretended she was a real person and we were best friends.

Henry gives the lunchbox a thorough sniff before wandering off. His disinterest in it gives me hope that I'm not on the cusp of discovering human remains. I lift the box, deciding it must weigh 3-4 pounds as my fingers fumble with the clasp. I'm worried I'll pass out cold from holding my breath before it finally springs open to reveal a small leather journal.

"Better than the alternative," I mutter while inspecting the cover. Slightly yellowed pages and a pristine buck-skin wrap indicate the journal could possibly be decades newer than the 80s lunchbox. It also could've merely been well-preserved by the metal box.

Who did it belong to? Why would they bury it in our yard?

As I open the cover, suspense balloons through me. The first page features a simple, "this book belongs to" with a blank line underneath.

"Wouldn't want to make this too easy," I huff, turning to the next page. Wide, flourishing cursive fills the lined page, continuing through approximately a third of the journal. Diane's cursive was sharp, and her letters were slanted. I know her handwriting as well as my own because I spent years reading it on the assignments she gave me before they finally enrolled me in public school. My dad wrote in all block letters, like on the back of the Polaroid, and only signed his name in cursive, which was too sloppy to read. So, who wrote in this journal?

My eyes scan over the first entry.

I'm creating a record of everything in case something happens to me.

Someone needs to know the truth.

Motherhood is everything I dreamed of and more.

Watching my sweet baby grow into a happy little girl has

been a joy unlike anything I've known. She's smart and beautiful and very thoughtful about others' feelings. She also makes me laugh every single day with her silly sayings and wild spirit.

When I was a teenager, I often babysat for a family that lived two blocks away. The husband was a doctor, and the wife stayed home with the kids, making it necessary to hire me only when the parents went on dates or the mom had appointments. Their two little girls were so sweet and polite that I never once yelled at them. I saw how much they loved their mother and hoped I would have daughters just like them one day.

What no one told me, what I never understood as a teenage girl, was the way a mother's heart swelled with love the first time she held her child in her arms or the first time a mother's toddler smiled up at her when saying, "I love you mommy." I love this sweet daughter of mine more than anything in the world—more than I love myself.

That's why it's so hard to stay, even though I love him with all of my heart. I don't think my sweet girl is safe when he's around. If he ever hurt her, I'd simply die.

The reason I say this is because I have evidence to prove he killed someone.

And I think he's planning to kill again.

Icy-cold fingers of fear inch down my spine. Who

is this woman, and who is the man she's accusing of murder? How did Nonna know the journal was in my parents' backyard? Did she bury it here? Considering she's never spoken fluent English, it wouldn't make sense. Did she witness someone else burying the journal?

Deciding I'll continue reading the journal at the airport, I try to refill the hole with dirt, leaving the remains of the bush in a pile on top. There won't be any way to mask the fact that it was destroyed. I shove the journal into my back pocket and return the spade and gloves to their designated spots in the garage before shoving the lunchbox underneath a tarp.

I pause to look at the spot where Diane took her last breath. If she had cared enough to tell me the truth about everything before she died, would my life be any different? One thing's for sure: I wouldn't be jumping on a plane to Baltimore with the only man I ever loved. I can't decide if that's a good or bad thing.

I make a note to ask Rocco if he knew about the journal, like Nonna. Maybe he'll recognize the handwriting. When I step into the kitchen with Henry on my heels, my knees wobble.

The conversation with Rocco the night before replays through my head.

"There was only one woman I was serious about after you. It started up a few months after I moved back. She had a kid from a prior relationship. I grew to love her little girl, but things got complicated, and they moved away."

The woman feared a man in her life would hurt her daughter.

"That's ridiculous," I say aloud. "Roc would never hurt anyone."

Then I remember his night terrors and the flash of his rage-fueled reaction when I ran into Nonna.

My stomach folds over itself. He's changed.

What if I'm simply blinded by my lingering feelings for him?

"You ready to roll?" Rocco asks, breezing into the kitchen with a military bag slung over his shoulder. I'm beyond grateful when Henry barks happily and rockets toward his new friend. It diverts Rocco's attention long enough to mask my startled cry.

What the hell do I do now?

CHAPTER 9
BEFORE

Josephine

think I might be in love.

Truth be told, I've had a crush on Rocco for as long as I can remember. It's hard not to like him that way, even though he's been my best friend—my *only* friend—since we were little. He told people we were brother and sister for the longest time until we started attending middle school together. Then something changed. He became a fierce protector and taught me to stand up for myself. I haven't been bullied again since the day I started sixth grade.

I suspect Rocco feels something for me because he started acting weird a few years ago. He gets all flustered, and his face becomes red a lot when it's just the two of us. It makes him even cuter, which in turn makes it harder to hide the way I feel about him. I think there's some unwritten rule we're both going by that says it's not okay to be anything more than friends.

Now that he's a senior and I'm in 10th grade, things are totally different. My parents aren't even half as strict now that I'm older. They let me go to school functions and out with friends. Rocco bought a car his sophomore year, and my parents actually let me go places with him. Technically, they think I'm riding around with Noelle Radke, my only girl friend. Whenever I "walk to Noelle's house" several blocks away so Rocco can pick me up out of sight, they never ask why Noelle doesn't pick me up at the house. I think they're just glad to get rid of me these days.

Diane has drilled into my head that it's inappropriate for young women to date and tells me I'm not to spend any time with boys outside of school. So when Rocco asked me to his senior prom and told me he'd pay for everything I needed, Noelle took me shopping in her mom's Aerostar van for shoes, jewelry, and a dress. She stored everything at her house until the big day finally arrives. It's a miracle my parents don't seem to know anything about my high school's events. I'm certain they wouldn't have let me "stay at Noelle's" had they known it was prom.

The dark-haired vixen and I became friends in 8th grade when we were partnered in a science lab. She loves to crack jokes and doesn't take anything too seriously. We bonded when I realized she didn't get into gossiping and didn't judge others like the popular girls in our grade would. She's an only child, too, raised by a single mom who's too busy chasing men at the bars to give her daughter much thought. My visits to her house would end if my parents were to learn the truth about Noelle's mom.

I'm so dang nervous when I walk over to her house the afternoon of prom that Noelle rolls her beautiful eyes and announces she won't do my makeup if I'm just going to sweat it back off again. Lucky for me, Noelle is really good with hair, too. An hour after I arrive at her house, I hardly recognize the person staring back at me in the mirror. The black mermaid-style dress highlights the curve of my butt, and the ruffles over my chest hide the fact that I'm still as flat as a ten-year-old.

It's so frustrating that I haven't hit puberty like the other 16-year-old girls. Noelle's mom once told me I'm probably developmentally behind because I'm so petite. Sometimes I wonder why Rocco hasn't asked me on a date before now. For all I know, he still sees me as his "little sister" and only asked me to prom because he was too afraid to ask a girl his age. I mean, I don't think he's even *dated* anyone.

When Rocco arrives at Noelle's house, my stomach sloshes uneasily as I open the door. Then I get a good look at him, and my heart thuds so loudly that I'm sure he can hear it. He's so strikingly hand-some in a black tuxedo, black cummerbund, bow tie, and shiny dress shoes. His dark hair is still long, but it's slicked back in a new style. And he's holding a bouquet of three long-stemmed red roses surrounded by baby's breath, tied with a black ribbon.

I'm most *definitely* in love with the man standing before me.

"Jo," he whispers, shaking his head. "You look… incredible."

"So do you," I say with heat spreading over my cheeks.

Noelle takes a picture of us with her mom's 35mm camera before shooing us away. "You don't want to be late for dinner at Bella's," she says as we head down her front steps. "Make good choices tonight, kids. Wear a condom!"

Whether or not Rocco heard that last part, he doesn't react when he opens the passenger's door for me and closes it after I'm settled inside. We don't say much on the short drive to his aunt's restaurant. The way he keeps wiping the palms of his hands on his pants, I worry he'll wear holes into the material.

Although it's packed inside Bella's, his aunt escorts us to a private table on the stone patio behind the building. It's a slightly warmer than usual day for late April, but a gentle breeze cools the air to a perfect temp. Since the restaurant was once a house, it's in a residential neighborhood surrounded by pretty gardens and lush backyards. Unlike the wooden chairs with checkered tablecloths inside, the chairs and table reserved for us are covered in white cloth, and there's a vase of red roses in the center. I recognize the silverware and crystal glassware from Nonna's dining room hutch. The dreamy "Fade into You" song Noelle is always playing on repeat drifts into the warm air from Rocco's boombox nearby.

Rocco's aunt, wearing a white dress adorned in colorful flowers and a large red flower pinned behind one ear, waits until we're seated before dipping with a dramatic curtsey. I don't think I've ever seen her in a dress before, and I've never seen her dark hair worn in large curls. "*La signora* and *signore*, your meals will be out momentarily."

"*Grazie*, Tita," Rocco calls after her when she dances away.

Giggling, I turn to catch his heavy gaze on me. "You're so beautiful when you laugh like that," he tells me.

Blushing, I lower my chin and place the linen folded on my plate like a flower onto my lap. Rocco has told me many times that I looked pretty, but his compliments today feel loaded with emotion. No one makes me laugh like Rocco, but I'm too embarrassed to say it.

"I've decided I'm not going to college in the fall," he blurts. "I'm going to work for Papá at the store until I know what I want to do."

"What?" I gasp. "When did you decide this?"

Grinning, he shrugs. "Does it matter? I thought you'd be happy."

"I want whatever's best for you. I get it if you aren't ready to start college yet."

"I'm not ready to leave you behind."

"If that's what this is about—"

"You said you want what's best for me? Well, being around you is it."

"Roc…" I stop to give him a long shake of my head. "That's silly. You can't just stay in Ames because of me. I'm perfectly fine without you sticking around to play big brother. Besides, I have Noelle. She'll make sure I get out of the house often."

He pauses to sip his water, then drags his tongue across his lips. "That's not what this is about."

His aunt reappears with a bottle of bubbly wine. "This is a special night," she tells us with a wink while filling our champagne flutes. "And you're with family. *Saluti.*"

Rocco guzzles his entire drink before his aunt makes it back inside. I take a delicate sip, trying not to laugh when the bubbles make him cough. I've never seen him so nervous.

Looking down, he gives his pant legs another swipe. "Nonna believes it's inappropriate to date a girl before she's sixteen, so I held off on asking you out. Now that you're sixteen, I can't wait any longer to tell you how I feel." He reaches for my right hand, still wrapped around my glass, and slides his clammy fingers around mine. Warmth oozes from his dark eyes when they lock on mine. "I love you, Jo. I want you to be my girlfriend."

Now *I'm* the one coughing. While I was hoping he liked me back in that way, I wasn't expecting him to be quite so blunt about it.

While I yearn to hug him and agree to be his girlfriend on the spot, I'm cautious. For whatever weird reason my parents have, I know they'd never allow us to be together. Hurting Rocco by letting him down easily would be better than all the crap they'd put him through.

"Roc—"

Rocco's grandmother and aunt arrive with two plates of steaming food and a basket of sliced ciabatta. I whip my hand out from his and clear my throat, hoping neither of the women noticed. As Nonna sets my favorite tortellini in brodo in front of me, her eyes fill with tears. After clapping her hands together, she bends to kiss my head.

"*Sei una bella ragazza,*" she tells me with a rare smile.

"Momma says you're beautiful," his aunt translates while serving Rocco the same dish. "I'm sure my nephew would agree ten times over."

"Thank you for making this night extra special," I

tell the women. "Your family has always been so kind."

His aunt's lips curl with a grin. "Most of this was Rocco's doing. We only prepared the meal."

"Thank you for that," I tell her. I turn to his grandmother. "*Grazie*, Nonna."

"*Si, grazie*," Rocco parrots with a respectful nod.

"We'll leave you two lovebirds to it," his aunt tells us before the women retreat to the back door.

My cheeks burn extra hot with embarrassment. "Lovebirds?" I ask Rocco.

He dips his chin, suddenly bashful. "I understand if you don't feel the same way about me. But if you do…it's time to quit pretending and start moving forward. *Together*."

"If my parents find out—"

"They *won't*," he promises with a hardened jaw. "I won't let them stop us."

Oh, the way he looks at me, it could melt an iceberg. Although my conscience begs me to say no, my heart's desire can't be denied.

I rise from my chair and move to his side to take his hand.

"I love you, too," I admit, my voice sounding incredibly small. "I think I always have."

His beautiful lips spread in a kid-like smile when he stands along with me. "You do?"

The heat from his presence makes my knees wobble. "But what if—"

His lips seal over mine, silencing me with a soft yet deep kiss, laced with layers of emotion. Tears spring to my eyes, and my head spins in the most delightful way.

I have no other experience with a boy, but I think something magical might be happening. I don't know how else to describe it. His arms wrap around my waist and back in a firm embrace. I sink against him, surprised my legs are strong enough to hold me up and haven't liquified like the rest of my body.

When he draws back, he frames my face inside his hands. I swear I'd float away if he wasn't holding onto me. "Let's eat dinner and go somewhere private."

My lips are numb when I smile, then nod.

Being with Rocco feels oh so right.

Like we were always meant to be together.

I'll protect our relationship at all costs.

CHAPTER 10
PRESENT DAY

Josephine

My lungs ache from perpetually holding my breath by the time Rocco parks at the airport. I didn't say much of anything after we'd dropped Henry off with Chris and his sweet dog at the gym. On the ride to Des Moines, I had discreetly reached out to Noelle, the only friend I've spoken to since graduating high school, and asked if she'd kept in touch with Rocco. When she didn't answer, I pretended to sleep the rest of the way so I could analyze my theory about the mysterious journal's origin to death.

Once we're past security, Noelle finally replies.

> Hello to you, too, stranger. Why in
> the hell are you asking me about Roc
> after all these years?

Considering she spent the better part of a decade training to become a psychiatrist, I make the decision to fill her in on everything that has happened since my return to Ames. I type back and forth with her, sipping on a tumbler of bourbon at the airport bar, while Rocco cluelessly watches the replay of a recent football game at my side. If he suspects I'm distracted by anything other than our impending trip, he does an excellent job of hiding it.

Together, Noelle and I conclude the diary didn't belong to either of my parents or Nonna, and she convinces me assuming it was written by Rocco's ex-girlfriend had been an imaginative leap.

> The journal could've been left by
> Rocco's aunt, a divorcée with two
> daughters five years apart, Noelle
> writes in a message. It also could've
> been abandoned by a woman who
> lived in your house prior to your
> folks. It could've been left by virtually
> anyone, Jo. Read more of that
> journal before you get yourself too
> worked up. Once you're thinking
> clearly, I want every last detail of
> what it was like to have sex with Roc
> again. Seriously.

With a roll of my eyes, I ignore her last request and continue to follow my current train of thought. The fact that Nonna felt compelled to tell me where to find it doesn't fit well with any theory except the one involving Rocco. But I keep circling back to the same two questions: how did she know it was in our backyard, and how did it get there?

"You're that girl," she'd said to me.

Was she remembering me when I was little, or was she mistaking me for someone else? Did the journal have anything to do with my parents or my alleged abduction?

When I think about the young man I'd made love to in his backyard the night before Diane died, I'm certain Rocco cannot possibly be the same man referenced in the journal. He's too gentle and kind, and has always possessed a desire to do what's right. Throughout my childhood, he was my protector.

But what happened to him after he enlisted? What if the horrors he witnessed overseas changed his personality until he became someone I wouldn't recognize?

My thoughts are so absorbing that I've become restless and uneasy once we're seated in different rows on the Boeing 737 in route to Baltimore. By some miracle, I find myself next to a middle-aged man who has no interest in getting to know the woman next to him. Either that, or he's aware of the paranoia surging from my pores, and he's afraid I'm about to snap.

After the wheels have gone up and a steward announces we've reached our altitude, I watch as Rocco reclines in his First Class seat and settles in for the flight.

Clicking on the light over my head, I dig through my messenger bag for the journal. Wild anticipation thrums through my veins as I resume reading.

I suppose I should start at the beginning so anyone reading this doesn't think I'm insane for loving a man capable of such violence.

I can't blame youth or naiveté on my decision to be with him. Anyone who knew him back then wouldn't have faulted me for falling in love, however. He was so charming and undeniably handsome. I suppose that's how he was able to get by with being a monster for so long. It made single, debatably naive women like myself trust him unconditionally. It made it easy for him to target his prey when a woman was flattered by the attention of someone with movie-star looks.

The funny part of it is that I had completely written off the idea of love before the fateful day we met. I believed it wasn't in my cards to have a traditional family, and I had embraced the reality with my head held high.

Then I saw him kneeling in the supermarket parking lot, scrambling to collect the groceries that had spilled from a broken paper bag, and it only took one look into his beautiful eyes before I knew. I was about to fall in love.

Things were wonderful in the beginning. He brought me flowers on our first date, opened every door for me, and doted on me in general. He was the perfect gentleman. That first night, he took me to dinner and a movie and paid for everything. He laughed at the appropriate times and held my hand during the last hour.

He left me at my door that night with a tender hug and a kiss on the cheek. I thought it was sweet that he hadn't assumed I wanted to kiss him. The first kiss didn't happen until we had been dating for three more weeks, and I was the instigator. I was afraid he thought I was a prude, and if I didn't do something to prove otherwise, I would lose him to another woman.

My mom was instantly charmed by him, the same way I was, and called non-stop after meeting him to check if we were engaged yet. He was often out of town to fulfill his job as a traveling salesman, so we didn't see each other as much as I would have liked. But every time he came back to me in the beginning, he brought either flowers or chocolates.

After several months of similar dates, we became intimate. Before long, he was staying at my apartment for a handful of days at a time. Although he was still away on the road often, he would always return for extended stays, and we would engage in endless days of love-making. Those were some of the best days of my life, filled with fiery passion and endless innocence.

Soon after we became deeply involved, the gifts he brought me started to change. By then, I was head-over-heels in love, so it didn't occur to me that there might be dark intentions behind his offerings. What woman wouldn't enjoy the gift of lingerie from the man she loved?

Until he brought a camera home one evening, I didn't suspect anything was amiss. How could I? He was the perfect boyfriend.

"Pose for me," he instructed. I thought I detected a hint of malice in his voice but quickly told myself I was mistaken. With a little smirk, he held the camera up between us. "You look so hot in that nightie, baby. I want to remember you this way when we're old and gray and have grandkids running around."

I covered myself with a blanket and laughed. "Don't be silly! You can't take pictures of me half-naked like this!"

There was something unusual about the way his eyes darkened along with his expression. It was as if I was witnessing an actual metamorphosis of sorts. But that would be ridiculous. He was, after all, just a man.

"I can and I will. Take the blanket off," he ordered in a deep, terrifying voice. His lips peeled back with a sneer. "Don't make me tie you to the bed."

With a sudden sense of dread, it was as if a boulder had sunk inside my gut. There was no sign of the sweet, caring man who had asked me on our first date and brought me flowers.

It was the first time I realized there was more to the man I loved.

Something dark and sinister.

By the time I started to think I'd made a mistake by choosing to become intimately involved with him, it was too late.

I was already pregnant with our daughter.

From the corner of my eye, I detect movement ahead. Rocco is speaking with a male steward, who in turn is looking my way and nodding with a sickeningly accommodating smile. I tuck the journal back inside my bag mere moments before Rocco heads in my direction.

I'm unable to stop myself from assessing his looks and attempting to determine if his looks are of "movie-star" caliber. I personally would describe someone like him as "rugged" because of the slight crook to his strong nose, his well-maintained beard, and the high swoop of his thick hair, although I suppose that's a commonality of most actors these days. In a long-sleeved blue flannel shirt, tan cargo pants, and leather loafers, he emits a laidback charm with every step.

Maybe I'm too smitten with him, like the woman in the journal.

"Good evening, sir," he greets the man at my side. "I'm wondering if you'd mind switching places with me so I can sit with my girl. I've already arranged with the flight attendant to pay for whatever snacks and drinks you want as a thank you."

His girl? I think with an audible snort.

The man awkwardly side-eyes me before shooting

to his feet. I slide into the aisle, allowing him to trade spots with Rocco.

"I figured I'd come distract you so you don't get lost in your own head," Rocco tells me as we settle into our seats and secure our seatbelts.

I've never been so grateful that it's literally impossible to read a person's mind. "I was just settling in for a nap," I snap at him, wishing it to be true. I'd give anything to slip into a blissful state of unconsciousness.

"Didn't sleep enough on the way to the airport, huh?"

With my arms crossed, I release an impatient sigh. "If you're expecting me to delve into my feelings on the situation with my so-called parents, I have nothing to say."

"I'm more interested in hearing what you've been up to the last couple of decades."

Briefly closing my eyes, I groan with the realization that it'll be impossible to escape him on this trip. Arms crossed, I turn to face him. "Only if you go first. I want to hear more about this woman and her child that were in your life."

With a shake of his head, he rubs his fingers across his forehead. "What do you want to know?"

"How'd you meet? Why'd you break up?"

His gaze darts across the aisle. "This isn't something I want to talk to you about, Jo."

My bullshit detector tingles. "Why not?"

He swivels his head, staring at me for a pregnant pause before answering. "Because Heidi claimed I was still too hung up on you to maintain a serious relationship."

I roll my eyes to the overhead bins. "Oh come on, Roc. That was ages ago. We were just kids."

His shoulders fall like he's disappointed I'm being so flippant. "What can I say? I thought you were The One. Can't help it if I never got over you."

Huffing out a sharp breath, I harden my jaw. It's the exact kind of response one would expect from a skillfully deceptive man. I refuse to be blindsided by his charm. "You didn't tell me how you met her."

"I was at the gym with Chris and noticed her from across the room. She was lifting twice her weight on the bench."

Relief rockets through me, closely followed by a visual of a woman with a ridiculously cartoonish build. "Seriously?"

His lips twist with a smirk. "Jealous?"

"You weren't bent over in a parking lot, picking up a bag of spilled groceries when you met her?" I confirm, clinging to his forearm with hope swirling through my heart. Whatever he says in reply, I acknowledge it could be a total lie. Especially if he knows about the journal. Maybe he's the one who buried it.

"Are you on something?" he spars with an unsure chuckle. "If you don't believe me, you can ask Chris about it sometime. I'm sure he'd love to rub in my failed attempts at adult relationships."

While I fully intend on giving Chris a call at some point to confirm the story, I decide his word is good enough for the time being. "I have to show you something." I release him to dig around for the journal again, then place it inside his lap. "Have you seen this before?"

He picks it up and glances at the backside before fanning through a few pages. "I don't think so. What is it?"

"Read the first page."

I study his face as he skims over the woman's confession. His reluctant expression deepens into a frown when he catches up to where I left off. "Who wrote this?"

"That's the million dollar question," I say, taking the journal back. "It was buried in my parents' back-yard. It's not anyone's handwriting I recognize. I haven't had a chance to read any more than you did just now. I was planning to finish reading it on this flight."

"It was *buried?* How'd you find it?"

"Believe it or not, your grandmother told me about it today after you sabotaged my plans by inviting yourself along. She didn't mention what exactly I was looking for, but she seemed quite upset when she told me something was buried beneath the roses."

He gives me a doubtful look. "Nonna spoke English?"

"I have a high-tech translator app…for work."

All at once, his face becomes void of color. "Wait. You thought the woman in the diary was talking about *me?*" Gripping the back of his head, he throws me a dark look. "What the hell, Jo?"

"The facts lined up. Nonna knew about the diary. You mentioned you'd dated a woman with a little girl. What was I supposed to think?"

"How about I'm not capable of killing someone? Your career has really messed with your head." He angles his body toward me and braces himself against the seats both behind and in front of him like he's prepared to flee. "I really don't know what to say to you right now."

"I'm sorry, Roc," I offer, touching his leg. Guilt

for what I've done makes it difficult to meet his gaze. "This has been a seriously messed-up day. I shouldn't have jumped to conclusions like that. My head isn't in the right place to solve anything right now."

Lips set into a hard line, he gives a disappointed shake of his head before he glances down.

Feeling as if I no longer have a right to touch him, I withdraw my hand. "I'd rather have you mad at me like this...maybe it was my subconscious way of pushing you away. It was ridiculous for us to think we could pick up where we left off twenty-some years ago anyway." Holding the journal by its spine, I subconsciously fan the pages through my fingers. "We're clearly different people. I've seen enough twisted shit since earning my shield that I've become hard...cynical. I'm no longer the innocent girl with a big heart you fell in love with."

"Wait." He traps my fingers inside one hand and points at the journal with the other.

"Go back a few pages."

I slowly skim through a set of blank pages until he tells me to stop.

The woman's meticulous cursive stops a quarter of the way down the page. There's a large gap of nothing, then a woman's name and a date.

MARIANNA HALEY
5/6/80

My heart palpitates with painful blows, frantic for oxygen.

The name and date are printed in my dad's unmistakable handwriting.

CHAPTER 11
BEFORE

Marianna

As I'm baking cookies for Lizzy and the neighborhood kids, I'm interrupted by a frantic pounding on the front door. Before answering it, I glance through the kitchen window and find her engaged in a game of hopscotch with Josephine and Cody. *Thank God for springtime,* I think as my shoulders relax. At least my sweet daughter won't be here to witness whatever kind of mood he may be in this time.

Dread creeps through me as I shuffle to the front door to unlock the chain and disengage the bolt. He storms inside with the finesse of a wet fox in a hen house with a ball cap pulled down low over his eyes. Sometimes I think he's embarrassed to be seen with me because he's always hiding.

As soon as the door's closed, he drops his suitcase by the door, then tosses the ball cap and his trench coat onto the sofa. The way hair's sticking up and his clothes are wrinkled, I suspect he's exhausted from the drive.

"Why was the door locked?" he snarls, showing every last one of his teeth.

"I keep it locked whenever Lizzy and I are home alone." Forcing a smile, I stand on my tip-toes to brush my lips over his cheek. "Welcome back. I've missed you."

I mentally prepare myself, worried he can hear the artificial cheer oozing from my tone. It's not nearly as loud as the thump of my heart against my chest. I've tried countless times to tell him we're finished. Each time he's given me the kind of dark, feral look that has convinced me there's a monster residing somewhere inside of him. I've considered running away with Elizabeth and taking on a new identity, but he's mentioned an old friend of his who works for the FBI and can track down anyone, anywhere. It's as if he already knows I'm trying to find a way out.

At least I haven't given him reason to suspect there are other men in my life. Had he known I was sharing my bed with someone else, I wouldn't be standing here right now, sucking in panicked breaths as I wait for his current mood to ooze from his skin and reveal itself. I've considered getting my other lovers involved and telling them the details of my situation, but those relationships have enough complications of their own.

He hooks an arm around my waist and forces me close against him for a sultry kiss. If I weren't so afraid of what he might do to me, I'd easily lose myself in the sensation. But I'm barely able to resist the instinct to push him off and vomit all over the shag carpet.

His eyelids are heavy when he releases me. "Where's my girl?"

"Outside, playing with her friends."

"I missed her, too. Why don't you call her inside so we can have lunch like a proper family?"

"They'll be done in a minute," I say, pulling him away from the window and into the kitchen. "What would you like to eat? You must be starving after the long drive from Virginia." With any luck, maybe I can distract him enough that he'll forget all about Lizzy. He can be so flighty at times that I don't believe it would be too hard. "How was your week?"

"Didn't sell shit this time," he grumbles. "Too many prissy housewives out there that don't want to part with their old man's money. Seems the more money they have, the less they want to spend it." He stops to sniff the air. "What's that godawful smell?"

"I'm baking cookies for Lizzy and the other kids."

"Smells like something you'd scrape off the bottom of your shoe." He digs through the refrigerator. "Where's my beer?"

"There should be some left behind the milk carton."

He cracks open a can and slumps into one of the kitchen chairs. "I've been thinking...we should move outta this dump. There're too many nosy neighbors around here who think they know our business." He guzzles some of the beer, then wipes his mouth with the back of a hand. "We need somewhere nice and quiet where we can hear ourselves think. I'm getting tired of the city. A man needs his privacy. A buddy of mine told me about an acreage for sale in Elk Neck. I'd be able to hunt deer and bear...put food on the table for you and Lizzy."

I cast him a tight smile, praying he doesn't notice

it's masking a boatload of fear. The women in the neighborhood have made it clear I'm never going to be part of their social circle. I can't say for sure if it's because they know I don't have a car, or because I wear homemade dresses. Maybe it's something I'm completely unaware of. All I know is their children are good to Elizabeth, and having them nearby gives me a sense of security. They may be prudes, but they're close enough that they keep a close eye on us. If anything were to happen to me, I'm confident they wouldn't hesitate to call the authorities.

Under no circumstances will I agree to move somewhere remote with this man.

Once I'm certain I can control the pitch of my voice, I ask, "If we lived in the middle of nowhere, where would Lizzy go to school? Who would she play with?"

"That girl doesn't need a bunch of uppity friends. And you're smart enough. You can teach her everything she needs to know."

I let out a slow, steady breath. "I don't know...I kind of like it around here. There's so much to do... so many places to take Lizzy in the summertime. It would be too far of a drive to attend the weekly street fairs and sell my crafts."

He releases a sharp guffaw. "You don't make

enough of a profit from selling that junk for it to matter."

"It keeps food on the table," I tell him.

He lifts an eyebrow in challenge. "Because I don't provide for you?" Eerie darkness pools in his gaze, giving him the appearance of a predator. "Who paid for this house?"

I stumble back a step. "I didn't mean to imply you don't—"

He springs from the chair, sending it crashing to the floor along with his can of beer. In two long strides, he's wrapping a fist inside my hair. "I'm the man of this house! If I say we're moving, we're moving, dammit!"

Sharp pain elicits tears from my eyes when he tugs at my roots. "Okay! I understand! Just please, let go. You're hurting me."

His dark eyes scan over my face before he mercifully releases me and shuffles back to the refrigerator to retrieve another beer. "Clean that mess up," he orders, motioning to the spilled beer pooling across the linoleum. "I'm going to take a long nap. When I get up, I expect a nice hot dinner to be waiting."

"Okay," I agree, adding a nod of compliance.

"I got you a real nice present while I was away. Can't wait until you model it later on."

A sickening feeling rushes through my gut. If it's something he wants me to wear, that means he's planning to take pictures. I force a smile. "That was very generous of you."

With a sly wink, he smiles back. "Anything for the woman I love."

Air rushes into my lungs when he slinks down the hallway and heads into my bedroom.

Silent tears tumble down my cheeks as I wipe up his spilled drink. *This is no way to live,* I tell myself. *What if he decides to start treating Lizzy this way?*

As I'm finishing up, the back door swings open, and my sweet little girl skips inside. She thrusts a plastic doll in my face.

"Mommy! Mommy! Josep'ine gave me one of her dollies to play with! She said I can *keep* it!"

Quickly wiping away my tears, I scoop her up into my arms. "Let me see," I tell her, taking the doll in my other hand as I rise to my feet. "Ooh, she's so pretty! I like her sparkly pink dress and her long pretty hair! She kind of looks like you with all that pretty blond hair! Did you tell Josephine 'thank you'?"

"Uh-huh," she confirms, bobbing her little chin. "An' I told her we're gonna have cookies later."

"They're almost ready," I tell her. "Why don't you

go play with your new dolly in the TV room while I get them ready?" I set her down and kiss the top of her head, inhaling her sweet scent. "Be quiet now, sweetheart. Daddy's sleeping in mommy's bedroom."

I've resigned to calling him her daddy even though I'm not sure who her father *truly* is. I can only imagine the consequences if he were to catch wind of my uncertainty.

"Okay," she sings in a hushed voice that makes me giggle. "I be weally quiet."

Once I've placed the cookies on a cooling rack, I check in on Lizzy to find her passed out on the sofa. My heart swells when I take a moment to watch as her little chest rises and falls. Her rosebud lips are slightly parted, and she's tangled a tiny finger around a strand of hair. I could watch her like this all day long. When she's sleeping, she looks like one of those cherub angel sketches, only far less chubby. According to the pediatrician, she's slightly under-weight for her age and shorter, too. But she's so intelligent and kindhearted that it'll make up for the other things she's lacking. I tuck the afghan around her before brushing a strand of hair away from her eyes and kissing her forehead.

My daughter is my entire world. It's time I come

up with a plan to keep her away from the monster in the other room. I'll die before I let him hurt her.

Sneaking down the hallway with my breath held, I peer into my bedroom to ensure he's sound asleep. He's sprawled out on the mattress, still wearing his shoes and snoring with the force of a chainsaw.

Gently closing the door, I return to the living room and take the liberty of looking through his suitcase. I'm careful not to disturb anything as he tends to expect everything to be a certain way, and I don't want to get caught because I've folded something incorrectly. It's filled with the usual shirts, ties, dress pants, and underwear. He'll occasionally pack a swimsuit just in case he stays in a hotel with a pool, but there isn't one this time.

Although I don't know what I'm looking for, maybe it'll be easier to feign excitement over whatever obscene lingerie he's brought me this time if I see it in advance. At the bottom of the suitcase, my fingers brush over something plastic. I carefully pull the plastic bag out from beneath his clothes. Before I peek inside, I already know it contains my present. I hold my breath as I drag the article of satin fabric out to examine. The camisole is fire-engine red with black lace details. It's exactly what I was expecting— tacky and nowhere near my taste.

Since it was rolled into a ball and shoved inside, I don't hesitate to hold it up to get a better look. Something drops from the center of the camisole and falls into my lap.

A Polaroid of a dark-haired woman wearing the same camisole as the one in my hands.

With a squeal, I drop the lingerie into his open suitcase and shudder.

He's planning to give me used *lingerie!*

While I've always suspected he's seeing other women on the side, I'm all at once relieved to finally have solid evidence. I could claim I was preparing to launder his things when I came across the proof of his infidelity. I expect him to somehow make it about me, but I'll hold my ground and insist I can't be with a cheater.

I grab the photograph, intending to tuck it back inside the camisole, but something catches my eye. Spread across a mattress, the woman's hands hanging limp at her sides. She's posed in a way that looks completely unnatural with one leg bent at a sharp angle, as if broken.

Upon closer inspection, her eyes appear unusually glossed, staring into the abyss.

Her red-stained lips aren't forming the usual pucker he orders me to make when taking pictures.

They lag open, lifeless.

A scream builds in my chest. I quickly slap my hand over my mouth to stop it from releasing.

The woman appears to be dead.

Vomit sears my throat.

I knew he was dangerous. I just never knew the extent of it.

Was he expecting me to wear a dead woman's lingerie? What about the other undergarments he's brought me over the years? Did they belong to dead women, too?

Will I be his next victim?

I race into the kitchen and spew into the sink.

CHAPTER 12
PRESENT DAY

Josephine

It's nearly midnight when Rocco and I check into our hotel overlooking Inner Harbor in Baltimore. The luxurious, 6-story building is clean and modern with a monochromatic color scheme and whimsical light fixtures. On the way to the elevators, Rocco swings by the hotel bar. Even though the cute bartender in her mid-twenties is getting ready to close for the night, he charms her into selling him an entire bottle of Woodford Reserve. Once we're inside our designated room on the 3rd floor, he pours the bourbon into two tumblers filled with ice, also provided by said waitress.

I stand at the set of windows at the far end of the room, eyes glazed over on lights strung across the mast of an old Coast Guard ship converted into a museum. On any other day, I'd be marveling at the peaceful serenity of the harbor and the mesmerizing way the twinkling stars dance over the undisturbed water. Since discovering my dad's handwriting in the journal and entering the woman's name into my phone's internet browser, I've become completely numb. Catatonic.

Marianna Haley was declared a Missing Person in August of 1981.

Her 4-year-old daughter, Elizabeth, too.

They were last seen by Marianna's friends in Federal Hill, a historically picturesque neighborhood in Baltimore.

After extensively searching for anything I could find on Marianna, I grew more frustrated. According to a news article, she'd been an artisan, known and respected for glass crafting of things like jewelry, vases, bowls, and sculptures. Gift shops and boutiques in the city had purchased a few substantial pieces but otherwise she sold her wares at street craft fairs. She also worked as an independent seamstress. Beyond that, the information was scarce. There was nothing on Marianna's daughter other than a grainy, black-and-white closeup of the girl wearing a party hat that had been used on her missing poster. The lack of details from the old photograph makes the girl seem completely anonymous. She could be anyone.

For the remainder of the flight, I continued reading the journal with Rocco at my side. By the time we landed, I felt as ill as Marianna had been when she found that Polaroid.

Was the man in her journal the same man I've called my dad for as long as I can remember?

Chilled glass touches the back of my hand. I discover Rocco standing at my side and quickly claim the drink he's offering. I suck it half down in one gulp. The sharp burn trailing down to my stomach does nothing to revive my wits.

"I called Nonna while you were renting the car," he tells me. "I asked her about the journal, but she was pretty confused...probably had another sundowning episode. I'll try again tomorrow." He pauses to take a long sip of his drink. "I also spoke with her nurse." Releasing a sharp breath, he tilts his head back. "She thinks it's time to put Nonna in an assisted living facility."

Empathy stings against my heart. "You have enough on your plate without dealing with my disaster of a life," I grumble. "You should've stayed with her."

"We're not going over this again, Jo. I'm here, and I'm staying," he affirms. "You're *positive* that's your dad's writing?"

He's probably asked me that a dozen times since our discovery, and it's starting to grate on my nerves. "Not without an expert's confirmation," I admit, still enchanted by the twinkling lights. "But I'd bet my life on it."

"The fact that he wrote that woman's name in there could mean a number of things." He slips a firm hand against my lower back and softens his tone. "I think it's too soon to assume he's the monster she was writing about."

"My parents lied about being from Arizona and it turns out they're from the same city as where Marianna lived," I remind him, my voice stern. "We moved to Ames in August of eighty-one, the same time she went missing. This doesn't feel like a coincidence."

"Maybe they were friends with her and promised to keep it safe."

"Or maybe they were covering their tracks. That

journal is evidence in a missing persons case. I need to hand it over to the authorities first thing tomorrow."

"She's been missing for decades, and the journal was buried in your parents' backyard for who knows how long." He drags his hand across my back in firm, reassuring strokes. "Another couple of days won't hurt anything. Besides, now it's even more important that you give it a thorough read from start to finish."

"I don't know if I have the stomach to pick it up again. At least not right now." The mere thought of holding the journal in my hands makes my gut churn with disgust. Was Marianna involved with a serial killer? Did he murder her, too?

I slam down the remainder of the bourbon and hold my empty glass out. "Keep it coming."

With a quiet chuckle, he retrieves the bottle and refills my drink. "You told me you found pictures of your dad when he was younger—right before they had you. Would you describe him as being handsome either back then or at any other point in your life?"

I pause to consider the question. "No, but looks are subject to every individual's personal taste."

"I still think you're jumping the gun by assuming your dad was the man Marianna was referencing.

Hell, we don't even know for sure that Marianna was the one who wrote the journal. Let's wait and see what your grandfather has to say tomorrow."

Remembering all the times I assumed something to be true during my investigation of Britta Baxter's murder, I shake my head before downing the rest of my drink in one gulp. He's absolutely right.

After polishing off 2/3 of the Woodford Reserve, Rocco and I complete our own nightly routines before we each crawl into the king bed. We're both wearing t-shirts with underwear when we settle in with a giant gap between us. Before I've had a chance to turn off the lamp on my side of the bed, his heavy breaths drift through the room.

With Marianna's name etched into my brain, I toss and turn for several hours before grabbing my phone and running various searches on my parents' names in combination with Marianna's and Baltimore. The results are limited to Marianna and Baltimore.

Around 3 a.m., Rocco gives me the fright of a lifetime when he begins shouting. Lingering guilt for thinking the worst about him forces me to wrap my arms around his waist and grip him firmly until he settles down and falls back into a dreamless sleep.

I pass out at some point and rouse with a crack of sunlight through the curtains.

I'm nestled inside Rocco's arms. We're facing each other, and our legs are intertwined. It's as if we couldn't get close enough when we'd both been fast asleep. In any other situation, with any other man, I would've bolted from the bed before he was awake and could register what was happening. It's the most intimate position I've shared with anyone since Rocco left for the military. I normally don't allow myself the luxury of being vulnerable with another human.

Rather than fighting it, however, I relax and let his warmth soothe my nerves. Maybe being involved with Rocco at this stage in my life wouldn't be so bad. As many times as I've tried to distance myself from him, he's determined to stay close and see this thing with my family through to the end. I practically accused him of murder to his face, and he still wanted to comfort me later when I became upset over my dad's alleged involvement with the missing woman and her child.

Rocco Giordano is a rare gem.

I feather a fingertip over his wide lips, longing for the days of our youth. Even though our history was laden with complications, we were blissfully happy.

Maybe this time around, it wouldn't have to be so complex. Maybe we could be happy together again. Content.

All at once, his eyelids lazily drag open. Our gazes lock. Something profound stirs deep inside me when I search his beautifully dark eyes. I suddenly want to possess him the way I had as a teenager. I want him to possess me.

He leans in closer, hesitating for a handful of seconds. With a rush of need, I straddle him and initiate a deep kiss.

While I'm in the shower early the next morning, Rocco tries calling his grandmother again. I tiptoe out of the bathroom with a towel wrapped around my body and gather my clothes for the day. As much as I try not to listen in on his conversation, it's impossible when we're sharing less than 400 square feet.

"Josephine Kelly," he says into his cell phone, using a slow, clear voice. The man should be sainted for his continued patience. "The girl who lived next door to us. Remember?"

He paces the carpeted floor alongside the

windows, glancing across the bay while listening to his grandmother's response. As hard as it is not to eavesdrop, it's more difficult not to appreciate his naked form as he boldly struts around with the curtains wide open.

My throat thickens when it dawns on me: I'm still in love with him.

"I understand, Nonna," he reluctantly says in reply. "Let them take care of you, okay? I promise everyone there is looking out for your best interests." The hint of heartache embedded in his words worms its way into my soul. I make my way over to him and embrace him from behind as he finishes the conversation. *"Ti amo."*

With a huff, he ends the call and folds his arms around mine. "The nurse was right. She's getting worse."

"I'm sorry," I offer, resting my head against his back. "This must be extremely difficult for you."

"She lived a good life up until now and took good care of me when my Papá couldn't." He spins around and grasps my chin with his fingers. "How are you feeling this morning?"

"Better now that I've washed yesterday off me." I playfully push him away before he can draw more emotion into the situation. "Go ahead and hit the shower—we can grab breakfast somewhere along the way to the nursing home."

In the time it takes me to get dressed, dry my hair, and throw on a coat of mascara, Rocco has showered and changed into a pair of dark blue jeans with a form-fitting sweater. On our way to the hotel's parking lot, a cool breeze rushes past, thick with the briny scent of saltwater and something rich cooking inside one of the several restaurants flanking the hotel. In the distance, a barge's horn toots, and traffic rushes down the street. Dark red bricks cover the walkway leading around the water's edge among historic buildings and more modern structures. A variety of blue and white collar workers rush past, sprinkled with a small handful of tourists, which I would suppose includes us.

Everywhere I look, the view is stunning, and the calm water somehow soothes my nerves. Although nothing looks familiar, I can't help wondering if I've been in this area before with my parents. I keep expecting to be hit with a wave of nostalgia at any moment.

Once we've grabbed breakfast and coffee from a drive-through, I help him navigate to the proper exits before retrieving the journal. Before I can begin to read, Rocco sets his hand on my leg. It had already felt like he'd forgiven me when we slept together this morning, yet the gesture seems even more intimate when his eyes briefly lock with mine.

"Read it aloud. Whether you realize it or not, I'm equally invested in this."

After clearing the emotional lump lodged at the base of my throat, I begin reading it to Rocco.

CHAPTER 13
BEFORE

Marianna

The next time he's away on business, I devise an escape plan. While I don't have proof he murdered the woman in the Polaroid, I'm unable to come up with any other logical conclusion. As badly as I wish I could simply grab Lizzy and run far away, I believe his claim that a friend in the FBI will easily track me down. The only way I can guarantee my daughter and I will be safe is to find a reason to get him locked away for the rest of his life.

One afternoon, while Lizzy is at the neighbor's

house for a slumber party, I head downtown to pawn my mother's wedding ring and other valuable jewelry left behind by my grandmother. I try to ignore the fact that they'd both be spinning in their graves as the greasy man in the pawnshop hands over a large stack of bills. While I'm not the sentimental type, I acknowledge the fact that I'm throwing away what's left of their legacies and won't have anything precious left to give Lizzy when I pass. But our lives could depend on the execution of this plan, so it's a small sacrifice that I'm willing to make.

From there, I drive the hour northeast to a realtor's office in Elk Neck. I meet with an agent who is more than happy to show me whatever my heart desires. After scanning over the list of remote properties posted on the wall in her office, I offer a cash downpayment on the least expensive one, and she proceeds to prepare the paperwork. The second I laid eyes on the dilapidated shack, I knew it would be the perfect setting to execute the final step of my plan.

Early the following morning, when he returns from a week-long trip to New York City in one of the best moods I've ever witnessed, my heart pumps at a rapid pace from the anticipation surging through my veins. If I weren't so repulsed by him at this point, I might have admired the way his complexion glows and his hair has lightened. I'm certain other women still find him attractive—the woman in the Polaroid surely appreciated his good looks before he ended her life.

"Hello, handsome," I offer in greeting. "It's good to have you home."

The stench of cigarettes and warm skin fills my lungs when he drags me closer for a deep kiss. As an act of self-preservation, I allow my mind to wander. If I push him away, the consequences could be severe.

Where could he have possibly have gone to have gained such a deep, lustrous tan? Somewhere tropical, like Mexico? Florida? All week long, the meteorologist had reported a series of thunderstorms ripping through the East Coast with a heavy emphasis on New York City. At this point in our relationship, he must think I'm a complete fool to merely take him for his word.

At least he won't suspect I'm capable of putting an end to his escapades.

When his hands wander over my rear, he withdraws. "Mary, you've put on some weight." With a hearty chuckle, his eyebrows rise. "You can't really be pregnant again, can you?"

Still encased inside his arms, I freeze. Did he

come across my secret stash of birth control pills? He has brought up the idea of having a son once in the past, but I've been going to the women's clinic to ensure that never happens.

Between the pills and the fatty food I've been binging in his absence, I've put on enough weight to ensure I won't fit into any lingerie he brings home. To keep him happy, I purchased a frilly, plus-sized nightgown from the second-hand store. If he asks me to wear whatever he's brought home this time, I'll offer to wear the nightie instead.

I gesture to the beading supplies occupying the kitchen table. "I was busy while you were gone, getting ready for the summer festivals. I haven't taken Lizzy to the park as much as usual."

The little lies must slide right past him because he's too busy glancing at the hand held behind my back. "What do you have there?"

I proudly present him with the glossy photograph that had been posted in the realtor's office alongside the listing of the property. "I know your birthday is still a few weeks away, but I couldn't wait that long to give you your present."

His eyes widen on the picture. "What is this?"

"It's a lot in Elk Neck…just like you wanted. Granted, it's not something you can live in full-time, but I thought you'd like to spend time hunting there. It would give you the privacy you craved. Maybe I could go there with you sometime." My stomach violently churns as I utter the last words with as much flirtation as I can muster. "For a romantic rendezvous."

I hold my breath as he takes his time studying the picture with his lips firmly pressed together. I honestly don't know what to expect since his mood can turn in an instant.

When he finally speaks, his tone is even. Neutral. "I don't understand." His gaze rolls up to meet mine. "How could you afford something like this?"

"I sold the jewelry from my mother and grandmother. I figured it was a small price to pay for the man I love." With a tight-lipped smile, I wipe my sweaty palms on my dress. "Do you like it?"

A slow smile spreads over his lips. "It's perfect."

Finally, something we can agree on.

———

The remainder of my plan involves time and patience. I continue to stuff myself with burgers, pizza, and ice cream, grateful when the scale rewards me for my efforts. Pangs of fear still cripple me every time he presents something new following one of his trips. *Has he killed more women, or were the items simply worn by other lovers?* Quite frankly, I can't stomach either answer. I'm only able to continue the charade, knowing I have to stick to the plan if I'm going to end things the proper way.

In the two months since I closed on the property in Elk Neck, he's spent every single weekend up north in the shack. He claims he's hunting, but he never comes home with any game, nor do I believe he owns a gun of any kind. Plus, I'm fairly certain the majority of Maryland's hunting seasons are limited to spring and fall.

A few times, he returns with the lingering scent of a woman's perfume. I try not to dwell on the fact for very long and hope that by dragging my plan out, I'm not sealing the fate of more innocent women.

Whatever's going on in the shack has been placating his desire to relocate Lizzy and I to somewhere outside of the city. Best of all, he's preoccupied enough that he's only around Lizzy for short amounts of time. It's a small victory compared to our overall situation, but it's a good start to the end.

Whenever he's gone, I spend my time documenting everything I know in a journal I purchased from a street fair. It's small enough that I'm able to store it inside a box of maxi pads—the one place I know he'd never think to look. Whenever Lizzy is either with the neighbors outside or napping, I'm writing. I write every night until my right hand cramps and my eyes grow heavy. After finding the Polaroid of the dead woman, I began keeping track of the dates he's gone in a little pocket calendar Lizzy picked up from the street at the neighborhood's 4th of July parade. It's critical I leave an accurate record of his actions and whereabouts.

As the date I've chosen to execute the final step of my plan nears, I'm filled with a crippling dread and oodles of doubt. So many things could go wrong. But I no longer have access to the Polaroid of the dead woman or her lingerie. The night he asked me to wear it, I pretended to have the stomach flu. The article of clothing mysteriously disappeared after that, just like the others. If I simply handed the journal over to the police, there's a chance they wouldn't take me seriously. Either that or they might call him in for questioning, and he'd become aware of my involvement.

There's no other way for this to end.

Hours before I've arranged to meet him at the shack, I take Lizzy to the new aquarium downtown. In the rainforest section, Lizzy watches in awe as exotic birds swoop over our heads, singing beautiful songs and squawking in earnest. I crouch down beside her, watching her delighted expression change with each new discovery.

Tears burn against my eyelids when I remember what I'm doing could go so horribly wrong that I may be leaving her in the sole care of someone evil. The most important part of my plan will come into play after we leave the aquarium and I take her to the neighbor's house for the night. It's imperative that Josephine's parents understand what's at stake.

I tuck a strand of her blond hair behind one tiny ear, pierced with a small gold stud. When she was three, she had begged to get her ears pierced like Josephine. I had finally given in, promising to pierce them if she used the potty like Josephine and stopped using diapers. I'd had problems getting her to consistently use the toilet and worried it was because being around "her daddy" was so stressful. With my offer, she trained herself and never used a diaper again. The day I pierced her ears using a sterile needle and potato, she'd been so brave that she'd hardly flinched. I can only hope she'll continue to stay brave no matter what lies ahead.

"You know mommy loves you with all her heart, right Lizzy?"

Eyes still fixated on a bright parrot perched nearby, she gives me a little bob of her head. "I love you, too, Mommy."

A hollowness fills my chest with the innocent trill of her voice. Will she grow up to have the same breathy lit as mine? So often, people comment that she's a little clone of me, having the same soulful brown eyes and sunshine-colored hair with a hint of ripe strawberries. My father and his father had both been redheads. Their genes had been so strong that both Lizzy and I were born with reddish hair that took on a yellowish tinge with time. I wonder if her children's hair will have the same reddish tone the day they're born.

"Mommy is going to a special place tonight to stay with Daddy. You're going to have another sleep-over with Josephine at her house. If, for any reason, I don't come back tomorrow to get you…"

With a sob rising in my throat, I scoop her into my arms and press my lips to her temple until the sob goes away. I commit to memory the baby-soft-ness of her skin, the bubblegum scent of her favorite soap that still clings to it from her bath this morn-ing. It's so unfair that I trusted a man who put us into this situation. If I had been given any inkling about the type of monster he has become, I would've run for the hills. But would Lizzy have still been brought into this world? There's no way of proving he's her father.

"You're going to stay with Josephine and her family," I continue in a stern voice while searching her beautiful eyes for a flicker of absorption. How much can a 4-year-old possibly understand in a situation like this? "You'll be safe with them. If Daddy comes to get you, lock yourself in Josephine's room and don't come out until her mommy says it's okay. I need you to be a good girl and listen. Do you understand?"

"Okay, Mommy." Her little fingers grasp a strand of my long hair as she nods. "I be good."

Before I can decide if she's able to comprehend what I'm saying or if she's simply understanding because she senses the man I call her "daddy" is a bad person, she slips out of my lap and tugs on my hand. "I wanna see the dolphins now."

Tears slip down my cheeks as I follow my daughter out of the exhibit.

CHAPTER 14
PRESENT DAY

Josephine

With a shudder, I close the journal and turn to Rocco. "Marianna suspected he would eventually kill her, too."

"I can't begin to imagine what was going through her head, but it's clear she was concerned about her daughter's safety." His eyebrows shoot up to his hairline. "Want to keep reading, or go inside?"

With a start, I realize we're already parked in front of a modern building with walls of windows and skylights. I'd been too absorbed by Marianna's story to pay attention to our location. The neighborhood is clean, flanked by new condos and a walk-in clinic. A large sign with sans serif print and a cartoonish sun boasts the name of the facility.

"Let's go inside," I decide, reaching for the door handle. "I need a break after that passage."

When we walk through the facility's double glass doors and start for the receptionist's desk, Rocco sets his hand on my lower back with the slightest amount of pressure. I've decided it's his way of comforting me without being too aggressive, which I can appreciate.

"Welcome to Sunshine Manor," a 20-something blonde woman greets us from behind the desk with a friendly smile and warm gaze. She wears a high, bouncy ponytail, and her teeth sparkle in the sunlight blasting through the windows all around us. She omits the energy of a puppy. "What can I do for you today?"

Untying the belt on my coat, I eye her name tag and offer a placid smile. "Hi, Sabrina. My name is Josephine Kelly. We're here to see Roger Carter. He said he'd arrange to have a visitor's pass waiting when I arrived."

The woman's eyes widen slightly. "*Oh.* Are you family?"

"I'm his granddaughter," I state without any

emotion. At this stage in the game, it feels as if I'm outright lying to her face. The way her smile falls, it's apparent something is wrong. "Is there a problem?"

"I'm sorry to tell you this, Ms. Kelly, but—"

"*Josephine?*" a deep voice interrupts. "Is that really you?"

I spin around to face a man approximately 70 years of age with a generous crop of gray hair and wrinkles etched deeply into his deeply tanned face. Around 6 feet tall and maybe 180-190 pounds, he's in excellent shape. There's a slight resemblance to the man I've always called my dad, except his narrow features and thick mane made him more distinguished. Beneath a wool trench coat, he wears a dress shirt and pressed pants that would lead me to believe he'd attended a Sunday morning church service.

"I don't suppose you'd recognize me," he tells me with a hint of arrogance hardening his jaw. "I'm your uncle Bill."

I move away from the desk to accept his extended hand, inwardly cringing with his limp grip. "Uncle Bill," I repeat, suddenly remembering a much younger version of the man standing in front of me featured in my parents' mysterious photo album. "It's good to see you."

"My god, it's been forever since I last laid eyes on you. I don't know why my brother and Diane were so determined to keep you away from us, but it sure is good to see you again." His thoughtful gaze swings to Rocco. "And you are…?"

Rocco gives my uncle's hand a firm shake. "Rocco Giordano. Family friend."

"Pleasure," Bill says before his eyes return to mine. "I don't know what finally brought you back to Baltimore, but I'm sorry to say your timing couldn't be worse."

I frown. "Excuse me?"

With a heavy sigh, my estranged uncle swipes a hand over his tired face. "I'm here because Dad passed away in the night."

As I hold the sorrowful gaze of the man who is most likely not my uncle by blood, Rocco's hand firmly sweeps across my back. How can my "grandfather" be dead when it's been less than twenty-four hours since I first discovered he was alive? Could it be something more than a mere coincidence that he passed before we had a chance to meet? Why didn't I drill him with more questions when I had the opportunity?

"Your dad died *last night?*" I wheeze through a tight pinch in my chest.

Bill gives me a somber nod. "The staff here is just as baffled. Dad was in exceptional health for someone his age, never had any issues. They assumed he'd live to be a hundred or more. I just spoke with the director and was assured there will be an investigation."

"I'm sorry for your loss," Rocco offers, probably sensing I'm too bewildered to form a coherent reply.

Dipping his chin in appreciation, Bill gives me a thoughtful look. I can't shake the feeling that he's carefully analyzing my every move. "He was a good man. I'm sorry you didn't get a chance to meet him."

"I am, too," I say in all honesty. The elderly man I spoke with on the phone sounded far too friendly and normal to have raised someone as cold and unforgiving as my father. "I was looking forward to getting to know him. I'd hoped he could shine a light on my childhood situation."

"I don't know how much help I'll be, but you're welcome to come back home with me and ask whatever questions you'd like," Bill offers, smoothing a hand behind his neck. "My wife said she'd make brunch when I returned. She loves to entertain, and I know she'd be just as excited to see you. We still live just a few blocks down from where you grew up in Federal Hill. I can take you by your place later on if you'd like."

I grew up in the same neighborhood as Marianna Haley?

My heart races as I give Rocco a tentative glance. His dark eyes spark with recognition.

"That'd be great," I decide.

While I doubt seeing the childhood home I don't remember is going to solve anything, it's one wayward puzzle piece of my mysterious life that will finally be set into place.

———

Carolyn Carter, Bill's wife, possesses a sunny demeanor and appears to be at least a decade younger than her husband. Either that or she has an excellent plastic surgeon. The way she carries herself with confidence and ease, head held high and steps without hesitation, I suspect she may have competed in a beauty pageant or two. She's a petite little thing with platinum blond hair. She wears a designer dress with designer heels and a diamond wedding set containing enough carats to blind a person from a mile away. While I believe her outfit confirms they had been in church earlier, I still feel grossly underdressed in a wool button-down top and jeans.

Although they live in a modest row house, the furniture and abstract paintings are notably high-end. The kitchen appliances and marble countertop sparkle with newness. The aroma of baked goods wafts through the air.

"It's so lovely to finally see you again, Josephine!" Carolyn drawls, tugging me close with a limp pat against my back. The overpowering scent of her floral perfume clogs my throat when she draws away. "Just look how beautiful you are!" With a dramatic gasp, she grips onto Rocco's forearm. "And who's this handsome stud?"

"A family *friend*," I say, inserting a slight clip of sarcasm on his behalf.

"Rocco Giordano," he tells her. "Nice to meet you, ma'am."

"None of this *ma'am* nonsense," she tells him, swatting at his chest. "Please, call me Carolyn." She retreats into the kitchen nearby and secures a white apron adorned with pink flowers over her dress. "Breakfast is almost ready, y'all. I hope neither of you is vegan or has any food allergies. I've prepared my famous loaded Dutch babies."

"Sounds wonderful, sweetheart," Bill praises, bending to plant a kiss on her cheek. "We'll get the heaters going on the patio and prepare the Bloody Marys." He points at Rocco. "Ever had one with gin, son?"

Rocco cocks one brow. "No, but it sounds interesting."

"You two go ahead," I tell them. "I'm going to help Carolyn get everything ready."

As soon as they shuffle out the back door, Carolyn begins directing me on where to find the plates, linens, and silverware. She's robotic enough that I wonder if my presence is making her nervous.

"How long have you and Uncle Bill been married?" I ask while setting the plates on the countertop.

"Forty-nine years! We began datin' when I came up from Alabama to attend the university here. Bill was already livin' in this same neighborhood—same as your parents."

"Did you know them very well?"

"As a matter of fact, your momma and I were real close. We were always together...I was pregnant with my Cody at the same time she was carryin' you. The two of you were thick as thieves when you were little." Forget pageantry; the woman was born to be an actress. She leans into dramatic pauses and fluctuates the pitch of her voice. "Poor little Cody was heartbroken when he learned you were gone."

"Where's Cody these days?"

Her complexion glows with a wide smile. "He's a Captain in the Coast Guard, in command of a maritime security cutter. We usually have to wait for him to get in touch with us because he doesn't always have the best cell phone reception."

There goes my chances of reaching out to him to see what he knows about our severely twisted family tree. "What was Diane like back then?"

"She was a real spitfire, that's for sure." After setting the cast iron skillet on the stovetop, she places her manicured fingers on my forearm and draws her lips into an exaggerated pout. "I was so sorry to hear she'd died, darlin'. What a tragic accident! Your uncle and I were all torn up when your daddy refused to give us any details about the funeral. I wish I'd known what we did to make them cut us out of their lives that way. I'm surprised your grandad didn't die of a broken heart decades ago."

"There wasn't a funeral," I tell her. "Just a graveside service involving me and my dad."

She covers her mouth to stifle a gasp. "Oh dear! That's no way to lay a loved one to rest!"

If you only knew the full dynamics of our family, I resist answering. "Did they still get along with all of you before they left?"

"Everything was just fine and dandy, or so I thought. One day we woke to see a movin' truck in their driveway. When I went over there to see what on earth was goin' on, they were already gone." She lets out an exasperated breath and throws her hands out at her sides. "They just up and left without so much as a goodbye or explanation and left the packin' to the movin' company!"

"You have no idea why they would've left so suddenly?"

"None whatsoever." The way she suddenly fumbles through a utility drawer without looking at me, I suspect she's lying. "Would you be a dear and grab the fruit I cut up from the fridge? It's in a big red Tupperware container. You can't miss it."

I retrieve the bowl from their highly organized refrigerator and watch her expression closely when I ask, "Did you know Marianna Haley?"

The pie server clutched in her hand drops to the floor. With a slight flinch, she retrieves it and recovers with a wry smile that doesn't quite erase the minuscule panic in her gaze. "Where'd you hear that name?"

"My mother mentioned Marianna and her daughter a few times," I lie. "I understand they went missing."

Carolyn begins cutting the contents of the skillet. "You and Cody hung around with little Lizzy quite a bit, actually. She adored the two of you like you were her big sister and brother."

"Were you and Diane close with Marianna?"

"Not exactly. She was a bit of a…*strange* woman… kept to herself."

"What about Elizabeth's dad?"

"There were a few men who came around in the time she lived here, but I don't if any of them were the daddy." She turns to face me with her bright blue eyes narrowed. "What's with all the questions, darlin'?"

"I don't remember anything about my childhood before we moved to Iowa. I'm just hoping something about being here will jog my memory."

"You were young. It's pretty common to forget life at that age." She scoops the baked dish onto a plate, then another before her perky disposition returns. "I'm sure the men are starvin'! Best to get this out to them while it's still warm!"

I wait for her to meet my gaze, but she makes herself seem busy to avoid it.

She knows something substantial that she has no intention of sharing.

CHAPTER 15
PRESENT DAY

Josephine

During brunch, Rocco and I engage in polite conversation with Bill and Carolyn. My uncle inquires about my career, and Carolyn's complexion visibly pales as I fill them in on my history with law enforcement. She's exceptionally quiet as Bill explains he'd retired from international banking 3 years prior while she continued to invest her time in worthwhile charities.

When Bill offers to take us on a tour of the old neighborhood after we're finished eating, Carolyn insists on staying behind to clean up on her own. As much as I want to call her out for being a coward, I decide it will be a good opportunity to get Bill's take on Marianna's disappearance.

It's not as breezy this far from the harbor, and the sun has taken some of the morning's chill out of the air. The neighborhood's narrow homes, built right up against each other, expand for countless blocks. Unique doorways seem to be the only thing setting them apart from one another. Their varied facades glow with pristine brickwork from a recent facelift. Arched windows and wrought-iron balconies complete the classic architectural design in embellishing details. Flourishing trees line the clean and crack-free sidewalks linking the buildings together. The idyllic neighborhood seems to be the perfect place to raise a family.

The three of us are a handful of blocks over the hill from Bill and Carolyn's home when Bill points to a row house with a cherry oak door. "That's where your father, Eddie, and I grew up."

"It's beautiful," I comment. "Such a charming and peaceful neighborhood. I can understand why you never left."

"Our parents felt it was important that family stick together. They encouraged all of us boys to buy a place nearby—even pitched in on our down payments. Your place was next to Eddie's two blocks up from here."

"Your brother Eddie? Is he still around?"

"He still owns his place, but we haven't seen him in years. He was always a bit of a nomad and never married. He likes to travel the country and sleep in the back of his van. Last I heard, he was out in California."

"Does he know about your father's passing?"

"Carolyn attempted to contact him this morning while I was taking care of things at the nursing home. His voicemail was full."

I quietly assess him, attempting to comprehend the dynamics of my father's family. For having parents who wanted them to remain close by, it seems they couldn't have drifted any further apart. "Do you have any suspicions as to why my parents left?"

Bill stops in the middle of the sidewalk. "I suspected this conversation was inevitable as soon as I spotted you standing in the nursing home." His eyes slide to the building. "I think it'd be more appropriate if you asked your dad."

My teeth grind together. "I would," I bite out, "except he's in a vegetative state from complications of a dental surgery. The doctors don't think he'll be around much longer."

Bill's eyes narrow with contempt. "Why didn't you say something earlier?"

"Do you really care?" It's a struggle to stop bitterness from seeping into my voice. "Besides, my parents were never the conversational type. They preferred to keep me locked up until I was eleven and pretend the five years prior to that never happened."

He clutches his chest with one hand. "*What?*"

"I have reason to believe they ran away from here because they were hiding a monumental secret that involved me in one way or another. I was treated like a pariah for the majority of my life. If you know *anything* about their decision to pack up and leave the way they did, I would really appreciate your candor, Uncle Bill. I've been forced to live with their dirty little secrets for long enough."

He runs a trembling hand through his hair. "Look, Josephine, your dad wasn't perfect. None of us are."

A stiff laugh spills from my lips. "What does that have to do with my parents leaving Baltimore?"

"I have a pretty clear idea of why they left. It had

something to do with his...*infidelities.*" The word rolls off his tongue like poison.

"He was unfaithful?" I raise my eyebrows. "More than once?"

Bill inclines his head. "I'm not exactly sure how many times it happened, but I'm pretty sure at one point he was involved with your next-door neighbor."

Anticipation gnaws at my insides. "What was her name?"

"It was Marianna Haley." His eyes become heavy with shame. "That woman who went missing."

I stumble back a step. *My dad had an affair with Marianna, the woman whose name he penned in the journal before burying it in his backyard.* It feels like the proverbial "final nail in the coffin" in regards to his involvement.

Rocco's hand glides slowly up and down my back as he confronts my uncle. "So you're saying her dad was sleeping with a woman who went missing around the exact time her parents fled Baltimore. You didn't find that suspicious?"

The wrinkles around Bill's mouth deepen with a frown. "I don't remember if the timing is right—"

"Oh, it's spot-on," I assure him in a tone that leaves no room for argument. "If you don't believe me, search her name and you'll find all the verification you need. She was officially declared missing within days after our move to Iowa." With impatience unfurling through my chest, I cross my arms. A tinge of guilt hits me when I notice he's looking a bit green, but I choose to ignore it the same way he ignored the circumstances surrounding my family's disappearance from their lives. "Do you know if he was the father of Marianna's child?"

Sighing, he drags the palm of a shaking hand against his forehead. "I can't say for sure, but I think your mom suspected that was the case. As Lizzy became older, the two of you started looking alike. Everyone saw it."

I lean back against Rocco's solid frame, needing to gather my wits. Whether I'm Elizabeth or Josephine, I may have a missing half-sister.

"Let's head back to your house," I tell my uncle. "There's something in our rental car you need to see."

Retrieving his cell phone from inside his coat pocket, Bill casts me a quizzical look. "It has something to do with your dad?"

"Possibly," I confirm. "And Marianna Haley."

———

On the way back to his house, Bill stops to point out several other houses with ties to the family, but none of them look familiar. I'm growing increasingly irritated that nothing has dislodged the smallest of memories. Our visit to Baltimore has only created more questions.

Upon returning to his block, we discover a police squad car parked at the curb behind the mid-sized sedan we rented from the airport and an officer standing beside it. Carolyn watches from nearby, huddling in a white pea coat and nibbling on her perfect manicure. Suddenly noticing the passenger's window is missing, I sprint the remaining distance. Rocco's footsteps pound the sidewalk close behind.

With a closer look, my heart sinks. My messenger bag is gone. "What happened to our car?" I ask Carolyn as Rocco and I close in.

"This is your rental, ma'am?" the officer asks, glancing up from the ticket book in his hand. He's probably close to my age with a shiny, shaved head and a bored expression. When I bob my head in confirmation, he scribbles something on the ticket. "Name?"

"Josephine Kelly." I rattle off my address and phone number, too.

He finishes writing a few more things before

tearing the top ticket from the book and handing it to me. "You'll need this for insurance. I'll file a report, but this kind of thing is low priority. Hopefully, you were smart enough to take your valuables out because it looks like they took everything not bolted down. Consider yourself lucky you weren't around when the break-in happened."

"Thank you, officer," I grumble, giving the surrounding row houses a thorough glance. It's the middle of a bright Sunday afternoon, and we passed several people out on a walk with dogs. Surely, *someone* witnessed the break-in.

As the officer drives away, Carolyn clicks her tongue. "This is normally such a safe neighborhood. I'm just grateful no one was hurt."

"Shit," Rocco huffs into my ear. "Marianna's diary."

"The pictures, too," I whisper, suddenly furious with myself. Why didn't I leave everything back at the hotel? I glance at Bill and Carolyn's front step, disappointed to see they don't have a video system on their doorbell. "Does anyone around here have a surveillance camera?"

Bill gives me a mournful shake of his head. "Like Carolyn said, it's normally a safe neighborhood."

Until someone trying to dig up old family secrets comes

to visit. "You didn't hear or see anything?" I ask Carolyn.

She wrings her hands together. "I came outside when I heard the police siren. The nice officer told me a neighbor heard the window break and mistook it for a gunshot. From what I understand, the poor thing nearly had a hard attack. We just don't see that kind of violence around these parts."

I slip into the vehicle on the driver's side and inspect the shards of glass piled on the passenger's seat. While it would appear from a distance to be a typical smash-and-grab kind of job, there's an unusual pattern to the glass. I run my hand along the dashboard, stopping when I come across a puckered hole.

A *bullet* hole. Around the same size as a 9 mm.

Someone *shot* through the window.

"Do either of you own a pistol?" I call out to Bill and Carolyn.

"Of course not," Carolyn snaps, tugging at her dress's neckline. "What on earth would make you ask such a thing, darlin'?"

Bill appears equally perplexed by my question. "Do you think we need one after this? For protection?"

Rocco leans through the open door to get a closer look. "What'd you find?" he asks.

Tugging on his sweater, I pull him close. "Arrange for a ride back to the hotel," I whisper. "I'll call the rental company and let them deal with a tow truck or whatever they decide to do with this. We need to get the hell out of here as soon as humanly possible."

"Why? What's wrong?"

"Someone shot the window out. They could've smashed it with virtually anything, but I think they were trying to send us a message. We're not welcome here."

"Shit," Rocco groans. "Okay, I'm on it."

When he steps away to open the app on his phone, I catch Carolyn and Bill frantically whispering back and forth on the sidewalk.

Everything about the day feels off.

If Carolyn and Bill aren't behind the break-in, I suspect they know who's responsible.

CHAPTER 16
PRESENT DAY

Josephine

The Uber driver drops Rocco and me outside of a seafood restaurant in Fell's Point, just down the road from our hotel. Floor-to-ceiling glass encased in black metal encompasses one entire side of the upscale establishment, providing an excellent view of the harbor. I inhale deeply, drawing on its innate peacefulness. A group of young children and their two chaperones wave at a small Coast Guard boat gliding through the center of the otherwise still water. An osprey perches on a nearby pillar, its whistles muted by the thick plate glass separating us from the outdoors.

Despite the chaos following us since our arrival in Charm City, I'm seduced by its vibe. Could it have something to do with my history here?

At the massive bar occupying the wall opposite the windows, we settle on high-backed stools beneath funky pendants crafted from blown glass. The bartender, a shockingly white-blonde in his late twenties with small gages wedged inside both earlobes, approaches us with a friendly smile. Over black trousers and a white dress shirt, he dons a black, industrial-style apron with brown leather straps and the restaurant's logo of a crow printed across the chest.

"Welcome to Poe's Perch," he tells us. "What brings you folks here?"

"Poe's Perch?" Rocco inquires, tilting his head.

With a smirk, the kid leans in a little closer. "The owner's a big fan of Edgar Allen Poe's. You know, the poet?" He gestures to the logo on his apron. "Thus, the crow. Poe lived a couple of miles down the road. If you haven't been to his house for a tour, I highly suggest you give it a try. I've never experienced anything usual there, but my girlfriend swears she felt an entity following us around while we were there."

"Interesting," Rocco grunts, clearly not sold on the idea.

"What can I get you?"

"Two double shots of Woodford Reserve on the rocks," Rocco tells him, keen to the fact that I've gone mute. Ever since discovering that bullet hole, my mind has been spinning with theories. I didn't give Bill and Carolyn so much as a goodbye after our ride arrived, but Rocco had thanked them for brunch before stuffing me inside the backseat of the crossover.

"Coming right up," the bartender says, setting a set of laminated menus in front of us. "I'll leave these with you in case you decide to order food."

Once he moves over the wall of liquor, Rocco squeezes my knee. "Are you going to share whatever's going through that beautiful head of yours?"

"There wasn't anything valuable in my bag aside from the journal and those pictures," I tell him. After decades on the force, I'd developed the habit of carrying my ID and bank cards in my back pocket and don't bother with cash. The leather messenger bag I'd packed only contained a paperback I've been meaning to read for months, a pack of gum, and the three items linked to my puzzling past. "And my bag was the only thing inside the car."

If it weren't for the theft of those valuable items, I would've been a little irritated about the messenger bag. It was a good hundred dollars more than what I would've normally spent on something so insignificant, but the wise saleswoman had insisted it was high-quality leather that would last for decades to come.

"Nothing else appeared to be disturbed," I continue. "It's a little far-fetched to assume someone used a gun for a simple smash-and-grab. And I had tucked my bag beneath the seat. It wouldn't have been visible from a mere glance outside the car. I think Bill gave someone a heads up. He was typing on his phone right after I told him about the journal."

Amusement shines through Rocco's eyes when he spins his stool to face me. "Are you implying your *aunt* shot the window?"

"Not necessarily, but she *is* from the South, and she became notably uncomfortable when I started asking her questions about Marianna. I suspect she knew about Frank's affair, too. It's possible they let someone else know I'm here...someone who's privy to the situation even more than Carolyn and Bill."

"Your other uncle?"

"Maybe. I messaged the tech wiz at my station to see what she can tell me about Eddie when she checks into work tomorrow. Since Bill claims Eddie is unavailable, I asked her to track him down. If he's somewhere nearby, I'd like to speak with him before we leave…see what he knows about my parents and Marianna." I drum my fingertips against the bar. "The whole situation feels incredibly off. Why is everyone being so evasive? I can't get over the fact that their father just happened to die the same day I came out to see him."

Rocco gives a little shake of his head. "Hold on. You think someone *murdered* Roger?"

"You heard Bill. Everyone agreed he was in excellent health for someone his age."

When the bartender arrives with our drinks, Rocco hands him a credit card. I take a sip of the bourbon, leaning back on the stool as the liquid does its magic in loosening my limbs. "Marianna mentioned buying a hunting shack. We could find the address by searching real estate records."

"What do you think we'll find there?"

"I'm not sure, but it seems a logical avenue to explore."

When he lifts his glass to his lips, I set my hand

on his arm to stop him. "You should go home. I know you're feeling protective after everything that's happened, but I assure you I can handle this on my own. I've dealt with much worse on the job."

"I don't doubt that." He places his drink on the live-edge bar top and threads his fingers through the hair on the back of my head. "But there's nothing back home that requires my immediate attention. Henry's in good hands. Chris can handle the gym on his own, no problem. Nonna is in hands more capable than mine. Everything I care about is taken care of—except for you. Can you cast your stubbornness aside long enough to let me stay here and support you for as long as it takes?"

The last text I received from Noelle as we were waiting in line to board the plane flashes through my memories.

Let him take care of you, Jo. Even if it drives you crazy. You two share a history…he might be the only one who can help you heal after all of this is done.

"Whatever floats your boat, Giordano." With a discontented grunt, I gently push him back against his stool. "But I draw the line at public affection."

Reclaiming his glass, he smirks from behind its rim. "Does that mean it's fair game when we return to our room?"

In lieu of answering, I chug the remainder of my drink and slam the empty glass on the counter before standing. I've made it two steps toward the exit when I hear the echo of his glass hitting the wood before his footsteps fall in sync with mine.

———

The shrill of a cell phone ring jerks me out of a peaceful sleep. I pat around the mattress at my side, expecting my phone to be in its usual spot. It isn't until my hand connects with Rocco's warm, hairless chest that I remember we're still in Baltimore. Once again, my naked body is coiled around his like a Bavarian pretzel.

I could get used to this lifestyle.

Disengaging myself, I rotate to my other side to retrieve my phone from the hotel room's nightstand. "Detective Kelly."

"Isn't it, like, ten o'clock out there? Why do you sound so groggy? Are you still *sleeping*?"

Recognizing the voice as the station's tech wizard's, I bolt upright. Rocco and I had both been awake for a few hours earlier, but apparently we dozed off again following another sinfully long round of lovemaking. "Good morning, Aubrey! What'd you find?"

With the unmistakable pop of bubblegum, I can picture the 25-year-old genius twirling her platinum blond hair around a finger while casting a bored look at her computer. Sometimes, I believe her intelligence is too vast to be stuck behind the desk in a police department. Other times, I'm convinced she's not sophisticated enough to work in a professional setting.

"That Edward guy you asked about isn't too far from where you are now."

"What? You're kidding."

"I wouldn't kid with you, ma'am," she teases. "You scare me too much to make that mistake a second time."

"You scare too easily," I spar back with a grin. Within days of meeting, she'd razzed me about wearing a T-shirt beneath a blazer to the station. After I told her the last person who had called me out for something was 6 feet under, she had gone out of her way to avoid running into me for weeks. "Where's Eddie?"

"He was admitted into a drug treatment center in Fell's Point."

"How long has he been there?"

She releases a dramatic sigh. "Am I going to get into trouble for this? I mean, we are discussing confidential patient records, and I'm assuming this is a relative of yours because of the whole 'Kelly' thing."

"Despite what you may think, I respect you far too much to let something like that happen, Aubrey. And I wouldn't be asking you to look into this guy if it wasn't extremely urgent that I speak with him."

"Okay, fine. Hold on." She hums a pop tune I vaguely recognize from riding the station elevators before she releases a little squeak. "Here we go! Mr. Edward Kelly was admitted…wait what's today's date? Oh, right. He was admitted just this morning…by another relative."

"Who?"

"Hold on…"

My impatient sigh finally rouses Rocco from his heavy slumber. He hooks an arm around me and drags me close, apparently ready to pick up where we last left off until he notices the phone pressed against my ear. Releasing me, he shuffles into the bathroom.

Watching his firm rear shift with every step, my lips stretch to their limit with a satisfied smile. For the first time since we've been reunited, he didn't wake with night terrors at any point. Maybe we really are therapeutic for each other, like Noelle claimed.

Am I too far along in life to become domesticated? Kids are definitely out of the question at this stage, but do I have what it takes to become a good partner to someone like Rocco? There's no denying I still enjoy solving crimes. Could I balance my career and a committed relationship? Do I still want to be a detective, or am I ready for a completely fresh start?

"Uhhh…found it!" Aubrey cries into my ear. "Oh, wait. I'm guessing it was *another* relative of yours. How many do you have out there, anyway?"

"Aubrey, what's the name?" I bite through a clenched jaw.

"William Kelly."

CHAPTER 17
PRESENT DAY

Josephine

Curbside, the treatment center could be mistaken for any ordinary residence in Baltimore. Much like Bill and Carolyn's, only with different colored brick and a more ornate front door, it's a charming rowhouse nestled in the center of identical units. Rocco parallel parks our replacement rental car a block down where several bars and small businesses disrupt the otherwise uniform neighborhood. When I ring the buzzer, a deep voice inquires the purpose of our visit.

"I'm here to see Eddie Kelly," I answer, injecting urgency into my voice. "It's a family emergency."

"And you are?" the man impatiently demands.

"His niece, Josephine."

There's a long stretch of silence. Right when I decide they're ignoring me, the door unlocks with a loud buzz. Rocco pushes it open, gesturing for me to step inside. Inside the building, a desk occupies a small cove beneath a stairway. The walls are painted a clinical white and void of any decor. After I produce my ID to the male receptionist, he leads us down a narrow hallway to a door marked 1F on the end.

A jolt of familiarity shivers down my core when I lay eyes on my uncle. Squatting on a velvet armchair, his gaze dances through the room's only window facing the alley behind the building. His knees shake with the force of a jackhammer. He's exceptionally younger than his two elderly brothers—enough that he could be mistaken for their son. He's also considerably more attractive than the two of them put together, with dark, wavy hair, stony features that remind me a little of Sylvester Stallone, and piercing dark eyes. Could he be the man from Marianna's journal?

"Hello, Uncle Eddie," I announce. "It's me, Josephine."

When he jerks his head in our direction, a montage of memories comes flooding back.

A man bounces me on his knee and tells me to blow out the candles on a cake.

A man kisses a beautiful woman with the same colored hair as mine.

A man pushes me on the swing at a park, telling me to look at the cute doggy.

A man hugs me and tells me he loves me.

With the memories, my heart skids to a halt.

I witnessed Eddie kissing a woman with features strikingly similar to my own. Based on the Missing Persons poster I found on the internet, I know the woman is Marianna Haley. Could she be my birth mother? Is Uncle Eddie my birth father?

"I remember you," I whisper in a trembling voice.

Rocco slides in closer to plant the palm of his hand against my back.

Eyes eerily vacant, Eddie Kelly's features tighten with a scowl. "I don't know why you claim to be my niece," his deep voice declares. "There's no way you're Josephine. No way in hell."

I stand more alert, eager for whatever explanation he has to give. "Why's that?"

The way he wildly gestures through the air, I'm *almost* willing to accept that Bill committed his brother because he has a legitimate problem with drugs and not because he wants to silence him like I'd originally suspected. I've witnessed countless addicts in various stages of withdrawal, and Eddie's performance is spot on.

"That thing!" he tells me, clearly agitated that I'm unable to read his mind. "The weird thing above your eyebrow! The clover! It's not there!"

"The birthmark?" Rocco suggests.

"Yes!" Eddie exclaims, all at once overly excited. He pumps both fists into the air. "A thousand times, yes! *That's* what it's called!"

Although I suspect he's still coked out of his mind, I appreciate that *someone* in my dad's family has acknowledged that I'm not Josephine. Maybe my theory of being abducted isn't so wild after all. "Why did Bill bring you here, Eddie?"

He stands and swipes at his nose several times. "He says I have a problem...a problem with cocaine...or *whatever*." He approaches Rocco and slaps his shoulder with the back of his hand. "I say it's not a problem if you're having a good time. Am I right?"

"Take it easy," I say, bracing an arm between them and forcing Eddie back a step. "I'm guessing you were high when he brought you in?"

"Higher than Mount Everest," he confirms with a wink before dropping back into the armchair. "If you're really JoJo, then you must know William has more problems than I do."

"Such as?"

Eddie throws his hands out like a Blackjack dealer when he elaborates, "Too much booze, extramarital affairs, getting fired, his crumbling marriage. Take your pick."

"Why was he fired?" I ask.

"He was accused of embezzling obscene amounts of money. To save the bank's reputation, they let him go in lieu of pressing charges. Ol' Bill walked away with millions."

Interesting, I think. With that kind of money, he would've had the freedom to stalk helpless victims at his leisure. "Did he tell you about your father?"

"You mean, did he inform me that Roger's dead?" Eddie clarifies with a sharp laugh. "Yeah, of course, I know the old bird is gone. Why do you think I took a bump? Nothing hurts when you have cocaine as your friend. It's all numbness from here on out."

Maybe Bill's involvement in his little brother coming here had been innocent after all. "Were you close with him?"

"I was never his *golden* child...that's for sure." He

mumbles something to himself while repeatedly stabbing a hand inside his messy hair.

Rocco clears his throat. "Do you have a history of use, Eddie?"

Grinning with the ease of the Cheshire Cat, Eddie asks, "Why, you wanna know where to score some, brother?"

"I'm just asking a question," Rocco responds with irritation flickering through his scowl.

"A history as in earlier today? Yesterday? The day before?" Eddie's gaze darts back to the window. "Hey! Did you know there's a *tree* behind this building? It looks a lot like the tree behind my place! I bet there are squirrels and birds and all sorts of creatures living in there!"

Rocco snags the side of my coat and leans in. "He appears to be in good shape overall, and he's on the heavier side," he whispers against my ear. "I ran into my share of cokeheads in the past...none of them looked this healthy or acted quite so coherent."

I nod in silent agreement. Eddie could be a past user who relapsed with the news of their father's passing. Bill could've slipped him the drug as an excuse to have him locked up before I could get to him. What other secrets is my family hiding?

I watch Eddie, deciding there's no better time to

extract information from someone who may or may not be lucid enough to spew actual facts.

"Eddie, do you remember a woman by the name of Marianna Haley?"

"Curvy blond with killer eyes?" He pauses to flex his jaw several times. "How could I forget?"

"How did you know her?"

His eyebrows wiggle. "In the Biblical sense, of course."

"What about Frank? Was he involved with her?"

"Frank?" He vigorously rubs the palms of his hands together. "Sure. As far as I know, anyway. Bill, too."

Rocco's eyes briefly widen on mine. "Your *brother* Bill?"

"Am I supposed to know a different one?" Eddie releases a hearty guffaw. "Pompous ass was involved with her for years before I found out. Those two had some kind of *arrangement*. Guess ol' Mary wanted to experience the sentiment of brotherly love."

"Gross," I mutter with a shiver.

"What kind of arrangement did she have with Bill?" Rocco prods.

Eddie scratches his head so hard that I expect to see blood. "I think it was something involving her daughter...Lizzy. He helped take care of her. You remember little Lizzy, don't you, JoJo?"

I respond with a brisk shake of my head. "Bill claims Diane and Frank left because Diane knew about *Frank's* affair with Marianna. Do you think it's because he was the father of Marianna's daughter?"

"You're asking if *Frank* ever fathered a child?" Eddie asks, releasing a stony chuckle.

"I mean someone other than...Josephine," I clarify.

"Frank's not Jo's birth father. The man's infertile. Always has been."

"*What?*" Rocco and I exclaim simultaneously.

Eddie throws me a scolding look. "If you were the *real* Josephine, I would think you'd know these things already. Your mother would've spilled the beans by now."

Hardly. "Diane's dead."

"Who's Josephine's birth father?" Rocco asks.

"How should I know?" Eddie's voice drops. "I missed out on half the things my brothers did back when I wasn't around."

Like the man in the journal, he was on the road a lot. I can't decide if he's reached the age of retirement, so I ask, "What do you do for a living, Eddie?"

"A little of this and that. Back in the eighties, I'd

sometimes play my guitar on the streets in the bigger cities. For a decade or so, I drove taxis. I worked under Frank for a few years, peddling encyclopedias to rich folks. I've done it all, baby."

Being a door-to-door salesman gives him the potential to be the killer Marianna spoke of in the journal. I cross my arms and cast him a leery look. "Do you believe that *you* may be the father of Marianna's child?"

He pins his shoulders back. "What does it matter?"

"What does it matter?" he repeats in an elevated voice. "What does it *matter*? Listen, I don't know who you are you what you're trying to prove by coming here, but I have nothing to do with her disappearance! Do you hear me! I had nothing to do with Marianna's sudden absence from the face of the earth!"

I hold both hands out in a peaceful gesture. "Settle down, Eddie. I never said you were involved with her disappearance. I'm simply seeking answers. If I'm not Josephine, do you think there's a chance I could be Marianna's daughter? Lizzy?"

"And they say I've lost *my* mind!" he shrieks. "Get a load of you standing there with your self-righteous attitude, judging me for being here! Lizzy's gone, just like Marianna! They're probably both buried in that godforsaken forest up north!"

My breath hitches. "The forest in Elk Neck?"

A young man in white scrubs enters the room. He's nearly as wide as he is tall. "I'm going to have to ask you two to leave now," he informs us, glaring at both me and Rocco. "Visitation time has ended. They shouldn't have let you in to begin with."

"Thank you for your time," I tell Eddie with a dip of my chin. "I hope detox goes well."

As we usher ourselves out of the room ahead of the orderly, Eddie calls out to us, "Bill was right about your parents, JoJo, or *whoever* you are. Your mom made your dad hightail it out of Baltimore because of Marianna Haley. Diane was protecting you from the ugly truth."

CHAPTER 18
BEFORE

Josephine

despise going home for the holidays. Everything about my life has changed dramatically since I left Ames to attend community college in Des Moines. Coming back only reminds me of all the reasons I couldn't wait to escape. I can't even say why I feel compelled to visit my parents, except my dad once made a comment about how I could show them some respect by stopping by because they're paying for my tuition. That's not exactly true, however. I pay for most of my classes on my own with grants and scholarships. I bust my ass, putting in hours at the campus bookstore and a burger joint to cover just about everything else I need since my parents only send enough to purchase my required textbooks.

There's one pretty significant reason I actually can't wait to visit, though, and he's standing at the edge of his driveway when I park my crappy old SUV in front of my parent's house.

Ever since Rocco graduated two years ahead of me, he's been working as a salesman at the sporting goods store his dad manages in the mall. Sometimes he comes over to my apartment in Des Moines and we spend entire weekends together. A few times, I've snuck back to Ames and we spend a night or two together on the couch in Chris's apartment. I don't care where we are, as long we're together and it's nowhere near my parents.

Flutters fill my stomach when Rocco catches my eye from his spot in the driveway and bursts into a massive smile. I know I'm biased, but I'm pretty certain my boyfriend is the best-looking guy in all of Iowa. Whenever my friends at school introduce me to their boyfriends or point out their crushes, I warm from head to toe with the reality that they're not anywhere near as good-looking as the man I love.

I swear he's even better looking every time I see

him, especially now that he spends a lot of free time working out at the gym with his friend Chris. His biceps and chest bulge against his long-sleeved Nike t-shirt, even though I swear he just bought it a couple of weeks ago because his other shirts were all too small. He started growing his dark hair out last year and his natural curls are becoming wilder. Now that it's down to his chin, he looks a little like the lead singer from Soundgarden. It drives his dad nuts —he's started referring to Rocco as "a punk." During our countless phone conversations, Rocco has told me he secretly loves getting under his skin.

The second I open my vehicle's door, Rocco plucks me from the driver's seat. He gathers me inside his strong arms and lifts me into the air. "Hey, beautiful," he croons against my ear before feathering his lips over mine.

I clasp my arms around his neck and allow myself to become a liquid puddle against him. I still don't know if what we have is extraordinary compared to other couples, but I swear I can feel the earth moving beneath us when his lips do their magic. If this is what true love feels like, I don't ever want it to end.

He sets my feet back on the pavement and grips onto my backside while deepening the kiss. I eagerly kiss him back, giddy with excitement and anticipation. I can't wait to tell him I started taking birth control from the free clinic on campus. We've been careful up until now, but I can tell he's paranoid that he'll have to support a family before we're ready.

"Get your perverted hands off her!" Diane roars from our front step. "Get away from her, or I'm calling the cops!"

Groaning, I pull away from Rocco and rest my forehead against his chin. Although we've taken care in sneaking around since I left home, my parents have known for years that we're together. Especially after they were aware that Rocco had taken me to my junior and senior proms. It's my mother's ridiculous comments and accusations that push us to keep our relationship under wraps. It's not the first time she's threatened to involve the police, either.

Part of me is completely over it. Why should I care what she says?

I release a noisy breath. "This weekend is going to be a total nightmare."

"You don't have to go over there," he reminds me. "Nonna said there's more than enough room for you at our place. She'd make me sleep on the couch, but she's a heavy sleeper. Papá, too." Slipping his hands back around my rear, he wiggles his eyebrows suggestively. "We'd have all night to fool around."

"Get inside, Josephine!" my mother interrupts. *"Now!"*

"We'll still have all night to mess around," I promise Rocco, standing on my toes to give him one last lingering kiss. "Meet me in your backyard at midnight."

When I spin away from him to grab my things from the car, I catch Diane glaring in my direction with so much hatred I can feel it in my bones. It's not the first time I suspect she wishes I didn't exist.

———

Later, after Rocco and I make love, we stay wrapped in each other's arms. Cuddled inside his thick sleeping bag beneath the tangle of bushes in his backyard where no one could possibly see us, I never want to leave. Between the warmth of his body and the fresh aroma of fall all around us, it's going to take an actual miracle to get me back into my childhood bed.

This must be what heaven is like.

"I think I've figured out what I want to do with my life," I tell Rocco as he's drawing circles against my back with his fingertips.

"Become my wife and raise our children?" he answers in a voice so seductive it curls my toes.

My throat thickens. Although it's not the first time he's mentioned marriage, the idea hits a little differently now that I've chosen a new path. As much as I would love to marry him one day, it's too soon. I know he's eager to start a family because he's older and ready to leave home, but the timing isn't right for me.

"I want to become a police officer," I say.

He rises to his elbow, looking me directly in the eye with a somber expression. "Are you dead serious?"

"I'm taking this class on social services, and we're talking about careers that work with abused children. I want to help other kids in situations even worse than what I went through. I don't want them to suffer in silence the way I did."

With a warm smile, Rocco sets his hand on my cheek. "Your big heart is one of my favorite things about you, Jo. I don't know how you became that way after everything they put you through. It prob-ably would've made most other people hard and cold. But not you. It makes me love you even more." He dips down to kiss me softly before drawing back and shaking his head. "But why do you want to become a cop? Why not a social worker or some kind of crisis counselor?"

"I want to look crappy parents like mine in the eye and tell them what they're doing to their kids is wrong."

"Maybe you simply need to tell your parents that now…get it out of your system."

"It's not enough." My jaw hardens when I imagine how freeing it would feel if I were to finally confront my parents. "I want the authority to take people like them to jail for their actions. I want there to be consequences."

"That's admirable, but there's a lot more to being a cop than saving abused kids. You'd be putting yourself in never-ending dangerous situations involving hardened criminals." Moisture in his eyes catches in the moonlight as he brushes my wild hair away from my face. "This is it for me, Jo. Being with you is all I've ever wanted. Nonna and Papá would be annoyed if we eloped without them, but they'd get over it. What if we said screw it and got married tomorrow? Would you drop everything and run away with me to start a family of our own?"

I half choke on a gasp when I catch his expression. "You want to get married *tomorrow*? And where would we go? Roc, I can't just take off before the end of the semester."

"Georgia." Running a hand through his thick bangs, his gaze averts mine. "I've been meeting with an Army recruiter and—"

"You're thinking of enlisting?" I sit upright and pull the sleeping bag over my bare chest, fighting back tears as I wait for him to look at me again.

"I've already signed the paperwork, Jo." He takes one of my hands inside his. "I leave for boot camp after the first of the year."

A profound sense of betrayal settles in my bones. We've talked about our future for several years. This was never a part of the plan. Shaking my head, I jerk my hand away. "When were you planning on telling me?"

"This weekend. I didn't want to say anything over the phone because I worried you'd get upset—like you are now. I'm sorry I didn't talk to you first. I want to do this because I think it will be the best way for me to care of you, Jo. If we're married, the military will pay for our housing and insurance in addition to my salary."

"I have to go," I mumble, scanning the ground for my discarded clothing.

"Jo—"

"We'll talk about it more tomorrow," I say with a firm shake of my head. "I need time to think. I can't do this with you right now."

"Don't be mad," he begs as I'm getting dressed. "Don't just take off without talking to me." Sadness strains his voice when he says, "I love you so damn much, Jo. We can make this work somehow...even if we have to be apart, so you can finish school somewhere other than Georgia. Please, don't leave!"

My heart physically aches as I walk away from him.

———

Later the next morning, as I hunch over a bowl of Fruit Loops, my eyes are swollen into slits from crying all hours of the night. I'm not angry that Rocco wants to fight for our country. It's noble, and it makes me love him a little more, even though I'm worried about him getting sent away if there's another war. I'm upset because there's no way I'm tagging along with him to Georgia. I've already looked into a police academy in Minnesota and was planning to send an application as soon as I'd filled Rocco in on my plan. Quite frankly, it hurts that he didn't mention *his* idea to me before making a final decision.

The possibility that Rocco and I might break up draws a fresh set of tears. I've never been into mushy stuff—I hate love songs and sappy movies. But I don't remember anything about my life before Rocco. He's been a pillar of strength through every milestone of my life. What would I do without him?

The desire to hop into into my vehicle and high-tail it back to school has been tugging at my chest all morning. If I'm not with Rocco, there's no point in being here.

I'm nearly done with my cereal when an ear-splitting wail cuts through the silence. It's so profound that I wonder if it's from a human or an animal. My dad's working for the landscaping business all day and Diane doesn't answer when I call for her.

I sprint in the direction of the horrific sound, flinging open the door between the kitchen and garage.

My mother is pinned between my SUV and the garage's concrete wall.

Her upper body is bent over the hood in a peculiar way that makes me believe her internal organs below her ribcage have been crushed. It's feasible to assume her torso has been severed in half. As long as

I live, I'll never forget the utterly vulnerable look straining her abnormally dull brown irises. Even though I hate her for the way she treated me, it's jarring to witness.

"What happened?" I sprint the remaining distance to her and hold my hands out at my sides as I assess the situation. I've never felt so helpless. "What do I do?"

When she begins to cry, her pain is palpable. "Hel' me...p'eas."

"If I get inside the vehicle, it might crush you even more!" I glance between my SUV and the door open to the kitchen. "I need to go inside and call nine—"

"No...'ime," she rasps.

With a rumble of anger, it occurs to me she's dying.

But she can't die. Not yet. Not until I know the reason for all the things she did.

I grind my teeth together, hands fisted at my sides. I refuse to let her slip away so easily.

"Why were you so mean to me, Mom? Why didn't you love me?"

"Only wan'ed...protec' you," she wheezes as blood dribbles from the corners of her mouth.

"Protect me from what?" I demand with a shake

of my head. "Why did you keep me locked up for most of my childhood like you were ashamed of me? What did I ever do to you and Dad to make you both hate me this way?"

"He was goin'...hurt..."

"Who? You mean *Dad*? Who was he going to hurt?"

Blood seeps into the whites of her eyes.

She releases one final gasp.

Then she's gone.

CHAPTER 19
PRESENT DAY

Josephine

On the drive from the treatment center back to Federal Hill, I can't stop revisiting the short conversation I had with Diane right before she died. Until now, my brain had tucked the memory away, probably because it's too traumatic, and I've been afraid to dig any deeper into the meaning behind her choppy confession.

Was she trying to tell me all those years ago that *my dad* was dangerous? It's possible she was referring to one of my uncles. Why would they want to hurt me like she claimed? What in the hell happened to me and Josephine? What is everyone hiding?

Outside of my aunt and uncle's rowhouse, Rocco and I remain in the car while I relay my thoughts from our visit to the treatment center. "If Eddie can be taken for his word in his current state, there's a lot of information Bill and Carolyn kept from us yesterday. It would definitely explain Carolyn's nervous energy when the two of us were alone, and I started drilling her about Marianna."

Rocco nods while glancing at their front door. "They must also know Frank is infertile…you'd think it's the kind of thing everyone in the family would know. That means Bill was telling a bold-faced lie when he said Diane suspected your dad had fathered Lizzy. Seems like a sloppy move to make when talking with a police detective."

"He hoped I'd direct any suspicions I may have in Frank's direction to take the pressure off him," I explain. It's a common maneuver made by someone with a guilty conscience. "With Diane and their father dead, Frank with one foot in the grave, and Eddie indisposed, I imagine Bill believed he could get by with telling me anything. He was confident no one would be around to fact-check his allegations against the truth."

"Do you suppose it's because he had something to do with Mariana's disappearance?"

"It would seem that's the case." I open the driver's door and toss him the key fob. "If you don't mind sitting tight for a few minutes, I'm going to do my best to extract the truth from the bullshit."

"It's not a good idea for you to go in there alone," he protests in a tone that's non-negotiable. "Someone already shot at our car. They might feel threatened and shoot at you next, and you don't have your service weapon. It wouldn't hurt to have someone watch your six."

With a blend of annoyance and appreciation, I nod my head and motion for him to follow as I step out of the car. "Let's go."

As we approach the front step, halfway down the hill, I spot Bill's white Cadillac that we'd followed from the nursing home yesterday. Whether or not they have another vehicle, I'm not certain, but no one comes to the door after I ring the doorbell several times.

"Maybe the treatment center gave him a heads up, told him Eddie's niece stopped by," Rocco decides. He glances beyond me to the edge of the building. "Want me to go around back and see if they're on the patio?"

Instinctively reaching for my weapon at my waist, I quickly curse myself for expecting it to be there. "Stay here to make sure no one sneaks out. I'll check."

I jog along the perimeter of the building and round the corner into the alley. Each rowhouse contains its own miniature backyard enclosed with identical tall white fences. I approach the fourth one down and discover the gate wide open.

Darting inside, I find Bill sprawled across the center of their brick patio, facedown and unmoving. At first glance, it doesn't seem he's bleeding anywhere. I rush to him, checking for a pulse, and note that he's still breathing. I gently shake him and call his name. When he groans in response, I do my best to support his head as I assist him in rolling over to his back.

His eyelids flutter open, and his pupils dilate as I crouch over him. "Bill, are you alright?"

"Josephine? Is that you?"

"Yes, it's me. What happened?"

He smooths his wrinkled forehead with an unsteady hand. "I'm not exactly sure. Someone must've knocked me out. The back of my head...it's pounding."

"Were you back here alone? Where's Carolyn?"

"She was just here. Why does everything look so fuzzy?" He tenderly pivots his head to one side, wincing with the movement. "Oh...*the pain.*"

"Do you have any idea where she may have gone? An appointment, maybe? Out to see friends?"

Once again, he brushes his fingertips back and forth along his forehead. "I...I don't remember. What day is it?" He releases a stifled moan. "Oh, my head...feels like it's going to *explode.*"

If he's putting on an act for my benefit, he's a damn good actor because he's showing telltale signs of a concussion. He appears exceptionally feeble, making it difficult to imagine him as a killer in his younger days. But I'm no fool, and stranger things have happened.

I extract my cell phone from my back pocket. "Try not to move, Bill. I'm calling for an ambulance."

———

After the EMTs load Bill into the box and the ambulance pulls out of the alley, Rocco and I stay behind to talk with the two police officers called to the scene. Officer Bradshaw is a husky man in his early 40s who walks with a purposeful gait and carries a hard expression that leads me to believe he's seen it all. His partner, Officer Williams, is young, possibly a year or two out of the academy, and continuously throws me a deer-caught-in-the-headlights look whenever I inquire about something.

"This wasn't an accident," I tell them. "When we came here to visit them yesterday, our rental car's window was shot out, and some personal items were the only thing stolen. There have been other questionable incidents since we first arrived in the city. I believe someone is intent on hiding old family secrets."

"Did you check the house for stolen valuables after finding your uncle?" Officer Williams asks, her eyes sparkling with inexperience.

"I wouldn't know where to start." I lift my shoulders with an exaggerated shrug. "I'll have the victim's wife contact you as soon as we're able to locate her."

"I think we have everything we need to file our report," Officer Bradshaw declares, flipping his notebook shut. He reaches into his uniform's shirt pocket for a business card and hands it to me. "If you change your mind and decide to file a missing person report on Mrs. Kelly, call the station at this number. I don't know how they do things in Minnesota, but there's no waiting period in Maryland."

"There's one more thing," I add, pocketing the card. "A woman by the name of Marianna Haley went missing from this neighborhood in August of 1981. I suspect Bill may have had some involvement in her disappearance. Possibly Carolyn, too. Would it be possible for an officer to swing by Bill's hospital room after he's declared stable to ask him a few questions? Maybe, at the very least, they could establish whatever alibi he may have for the dates related to Ms. Haley's disappearance."

Officer Williams gives me a quick once-over before batting her long eyelashes. "I would think you're qualified for that job, Detective."

"He's family, and he's already fed me countless lies," I explain. "I'd rather a uniformed officer blind-side him when he's least expecting it."

"Understood," Officer Bradshaw replies with a curt nod. "I'll run it by our Captain and see what we can do."

I shake his hand, then hers. "Thank you, Officers. I imagine our stay here has been extended by at least another day, so if you come up with any more ques-tions, feel free to contact me using the number I provided with my statement."

Rocco and I stand shoulder-to-shoulder, watching as they depart. Air deflates from my lungs once they're out of sight. "I don't like how any of this is going down. It's almost as if someone has been watching our every move since we arrived in Baltimore. Where the hell did Carolyn go? Did someone kidnap her, or did she do this to Bill?"

Rocco wraps his thick arm around my waist and pulls me close enough to kiss the top of my head. "Breathe, Jo. You'll figure it all out with time."

"What if I don't? What if Marianna—the woman who could very possibly be my birth mother—stays missing? What if her body is never found? Whatever they did...whatever *my family* did...she deserves justice." I press my forehead against his chest, feeling an instant surge of relief when he cocoons me in his arms.

"Let's grab a drink and something to eat from the same place we stopped yesterday. They had a great menu with fresh seafood. I bet you'll think a little more clearly with a full stomach."

"As wonderful as that sounds, let's put it off until later tonight. We can grab something from a drive-through on our way out of town."

His eyebrows lift. "Where are we going?"

"It's time we pay a visit to Marianna's shack in Elk Neck."

An hour north of the city, when we locate the property listed on public records as still belonging to Marianna Haley, we come across a dirt road. Nestled inside a dense forest of varied hardwoods, evergreens, and shrubs, scrub trees, and waist-high weeds bombard the crude road. Rocco parks at the road's entrance.

I retrieve my coat from the backseat and open my door. "Guess we walk from here."

Other than the occasional rustle of animals scurrying through bushes, the crunch of our boots on the variegated terrain is the only sound to break the silence. I've had near-perfect hearing for most of my life, but when I stop to listen, I'm unnerved by the lack of noise. It's like the forest is swallowing everything whole.

"It's almost too quiet here," I comment, slightly startled by the sound of my own voice.

"It's the perfect place to bury old secrets." His fingers slide around mine, giving them a tentative squeeze. "After we leave here, what do you think you'll do?"

"If you're asking how soon I'm going to head back to Chaska—"

"I mean, what will you do about your dad...*Frank*. Are you going to confront him about the infertility thing?"

"Telling him what I know wouldn't do much good. He's non-responsive. The nurses I spoke with after visiting with him told me they'd be surprised if he made it through the weekend. They said they'd reach out if there were any changes—good or bad. The fact that they haven't called yet..." I shrug. "Either way, it doesn't really matter."

"Do you think you'll take a DNA test?"

I consider the question. At this point in my life, I've accepted that I'll never have a family I can count on. After learning about the Kelly family secrets since coming to Baltimore, I'd be more than happy if things were to remain that way.

Highlighted beneath the afternoon sun's strong rays, a little building comes in to view half a dozen or so yards ahead. It's small enough and in such an advanced state of disrepair that I'm able to appreciate why everyone calls it a shack as opposed to a cabin. The wood siding has rotted out in places and it's leaning to one side.

I drop Rocco's hand to point it out to him. "I think that's it. That's the place." I quicken my pace to a faster clip before I break into a jog.

"Jo, wait up!" Rocco calls out before grunting and swearing behind me. I glance over my shoulder to find him on the ground, struggling to release a complicated tangle of vines from around his boot.

"I'll meet you there!" Adrenaline propels me forward. If Marianna left any other clues as to the identity of the alleged killer, they'd certainly be here. Sometimes it feels as if the truth is within grasp. Ever since I found Bill unconscious, I swear it's no closer than it had been before I made the trip down to Ames.

I burst through the shack's open door, giving the four walls a thorough scan. The place is empty save for a double bed in one corner, and smells mustier than the forest. I lift the mattress to check for any hidden items before dragging the entire bed away from the wall. The building's interior has decayed as much as the outside, leaving gaping holes in the floorboards as well. One board sticks out from the others with a darker stain and mismatched grain pattern.

"Bingo," I whisper, bending to pry it up.

Nestled inside a little cubby, I discover the journal and the photographs taken from our rental car.

Who put them here? I wonder as I extract them.

The sound of footsteps fall on the floorboards behind me, each one getting louder and closer. Before I have a chance to spin around and tell Rocco what I've discovered, I feel the cold touch of metal against the back of my head. My heart races as I try to speak, but the words get stuck in my throat. My mind races as I realize the gravity of the situation. Every second feels like an eternity, waiting for the inevitable click of the trigger.

CHAPTER 20
PRESENT DAY

Marianna

Despite Lizzy's close friendship with Josephine, her mother has never warmed to me. I get the impression she isn't a friendly person in general. She seems the type to walk into a party and decide with a single glance that she's better than everyone else in attendance. She's not particularly attractive, though she's overly tall enough for a woman to demand attention when she enters a room.

At least she makes an effort to get along with the other mothers. Every time I drop Lizzy for a sleep-over, I'm met with a cold, contentious stare that she attempts to mask with a stiff smile.

She may as well outright accuse me of sleeping with her husband. It's not like I could blame her or the other women in the neighborhood for treating me like a harlot.

I've rightfully earned the reputation.

It was never my intention to start affairs with married men, even though it was a behavior I may have unintentionally picked up from my mother. My interactions with them always started with a friendly wave or a polite conversation about the weather. Before I moved to Federal Hill, they'd usually offer to fix something inside my apartment they claimed needed attention or "bump into me" while on my weekly visit to the grocery store. After Lizzy was born, they'd sometimes stop in to chat while our children were playing together or sneak over while their wives were away to see if I knew where to score good weed. One time, I woke to find one sleeping in my backyard after a fight with his wife. The seemingly innocent excuses were endless.

I never initiated anything. But once they started offering the kind of attention I failed to get elsewhere, I could not resist.

Married men have always revered me as extraordinarily attractive. Maybe it's because their wives are settled in their roles as caretakers, and they've become blind to how good they have it at home. Maybe it's because they grow bored with the same woman. I suppose it could be my carefree spirit and the fact that I'm oblivious to social norms and fashion trends. I'm not exactly sure. All I know is they enjoy putting me on a pedestal and spoiling me like a princess.

If a married man hadn't offered to set me up in his neighborhood shortly after discovering I may be carrying his child, I would not have been able to afford my rowhouse. Looking back at the situation, I suppose it was his way of ensuring I remained a kept woman. He obviously enjoyed the benefits of sleeping with a younger woman and wanted to keep me close. I suppose it was also his way of bribing me so I wouldn't spill the beans to his wife.

As I stand with Lizzy on Josephine's front step, intending to drop her off for what could be the final time, Josephine's mom answers the door with the same cool stare I've come to expect.

I crouch at Lizzy's side to kiss her cheek. The way she clutches the pink mouse I made when she was born gives her a more youthful appearance. I try not to dwell on the idea of never seeing her again.

"Remember what mommy said," I whisper, drawing her into my arms for a brief hug. "Be a good girl, and listen to Josephine's mommy."

"I will," she promises, beaming at the sight of her friend peering out behind her mom. She pulls away from me, calling over her shoulder, "Love you, mommy!"

"I love you too, sweet girl!" Fighting through a rush of tears, I rise to my feet and look Josephine's mom in the eye. "Can I have a minute of your time before I go?"

"I'm listening," she bites out.

"Out here, where the girls can't overhear us."

Her mouth becomes as rigid as stone when she glances into the house where the girls are already playing with Josephine's dolls. "I suppose that would be okay," she decides, stepping onto the front step and firmly closing the door behind her. She crosses her arms, impatiently waiting for me to speak.

Something icky and hot, like embarrassment, floods through my limbs. Even if I were to apologize for everything I've done, I doubt she could muster the will to forgive me. "I...um...just wanted to let you know we're spending the night in Elk Neck. I bought a property a few miles off the main highway, straight east of the hair salon at the edge of town. It's a small shack, barely visible from the highway."

"Sounds romantic," she replies in a clipped tone. "Anything else?"

I shift my weight, wishing I could disappear so I wouldn't have to feel the weight of her judgment. "In case I don't show up in the morning—"

Her judgmental gaze sharpens. "Are you planning to *abandon* your daughter?"

"No. *Never*," I swear. "I love that little girl with all my heart. It's just...there's something important in her overnight bag, wrapped in the quilt I made her that she can't sleep without. Promise me you'll protect it with your life. If I disappear, I need you to turn it over to the proper authorities."

"What is it?"

"You'll know what it is when you see it."

With a roll of her eyes, she lets out a disapproving *tsk*. "I don't know what kind of game you're playing—"

I forcefully grip her forearm. "I need you to promise you won't release her to her father, no matter what."

"You're *hurting* me," she snarls, attempting to pry my fingers loose.

"Please," I beg through a rush of tears. "I value

her life more than my own. Surely, as a parent, you can relate to that feeling. Promise you'll protect her like she's yours."

Holding my desperate stare, her angry expression begins to fade and her defensive posture relaxes. For a sliver of a moment, I feel a connection form between us—*mother to mother.*

She abandons her efforts to release my hand and gives a definitive dip of her chin. "Okay, Marianna. I promise to protect her at all costs."

When I begin to retract my arm, she holds it in place and gives me a stern look. "If you're in some kind of danger—"

"You can't get involved," I say, yanking away from her. "It's not safe."

Her lips peel back with a sneer. "*Marianna—*"

"There's only one way this can end," I interrupt with a firm head shake.

Too choked up to say anything more, I walk away.

———

"You're late," he tells me as I enter with an armload of groceries. He's sitting on the edge of the shack's only furniture—a worn cot—in nothing more than his underwear and a white undershirt. Although it's abnormally cold this time of year, sweat drips down his face and stains the shirt's armpits.

Until my headlights swept over the dark shadow of Mauldin Mountain, I was at peace with the decisions that led me here. Josephine's mom seemed devoted to protecting Lizzy, and I'm about to ensure no other women will have to suffer at his hands again. But something about the combination of rocks and trees on the steep slopes ahead made it hard to breathe. Finding him in a foul mood only adds to my growing trepidation.

"The first place I stopped didn't carry your beer," I lie, handing him the six-pack of cans. As I cross the floor to close the only window, he cracks open one of the cans. "My lord! A polar bear could live in here!"

A beat of silence passes before he speaks. "I had an interesting conversation with my brother this morning." His voice drips with cold anger as he rises from the cot. I'm frozen with blinding fear as he shuffles over to where I stand. "He was telling me all about this hot piece of ass he's been sleeping with...said she lives right down the block from him."

Too late to turn back now. "Your brother is nicer than you'll ever me," I sneer with a defiant lift of my chin. "He's never hit me."

His body odor assaults my senses when he leans in. "So you aren't going to deny it's true?"

"I know what you're doing when you're not with me," I confess, digging my fingernails into the palms of my hands. "I know there are other women. I can smell their perfume."

"You caught me red-handed," he admits with a hard laugh. "What are you going to do about it?"

My stomach clenches when I blurt, "I saw the Polaroid you took…of a *dead woman*. She was wearing the exact same lingerie you brought home for me to wear. The night I pretended to be sick…I dug through your suitcase while you were sleeping."

"You *saw a Polaroid?*" he mocks, attempting to match my tone. If he is indeed guilty, I don't detect the slightest acknowledgment in his body language. He remains as cool as a cucumber even though he's sweating profusely. "What does that prove?"

"How many women have you killed?"

A smile curls the edges of his lips. "Killed?"

"Where do you go when you tell me you're on the road? Do you meet them in bars or murder them in their own homes? How do you lure them away? How do you get them to trust you?"

"You're talking nonsense. I've been good to you, Mary…given you everything you've ever wanted.

How could you think I would do such a thing? I work hard to provide for you and our daughter."

"Lizzy is not *your* daughter."

Darkness spreads across his expression as he stumbles back like he was punched. "Is that so?"

"I tracked my cycle...she was conceived while you were on one of your 'trips'."

"You're lying." Sneering, he stalks back toward me. "You can't know that for certain."

I stand firm on my feet, determined to see this plan through to the end. I won't back down. Those poor women deserve justice.

"Tell me the truth about the woman in the Polaroid, and I'll tell you the truth about her. How many others were there?"

His eyes darken, revealing the monster buried inside. "You really wanna know?"

My throat tightens as he stalks nearer.

"The woman you saw in that Polaroid was number four."

"No," I rasp, giving a slight shake of my head. "That can't be true."

"There have been at least a dozen since," he claims with a smirk that gives him a fun-house-like appearance. "Honestly, I've lost count. It's become more than a hobby. And you made it so much easier by giving me this place."

"What do you mean?"

"You gifted me with acres of unlimited possibilities. Most people don't know how easy it is to cross state lines with a body in the trunk of a car. No more worrying about how I'm going to dispose of their bodies once I'm done."

Dread trickles down my spine like acid.

"You monster!" I shriek.

He raises a hand to strike me, but I deflect it mid-air by taking a large stride back. "I'm done taking your abuse. I'm leaving you, and I'm going to tell the police everything I know. You'll never see Lizzy again because you're going to spend the rest of your life behind bars."

"Like hell I am," he snarls, drawing a large knife into the air between us. "You're not stepping foot outside this cabin."

With my last trembling breath, I spot a set of headlights cutting through the trees.

CHAPTER 21
PRESENT DAY

Josephine

My heartbeat wallops with irregularity as I try to work out who would be aiming a gun at my head, ready to fire. Did someone follow us from Federal Hill? Were they already here, waiting? Red-hot panic slithers through my belly. *Where's Rocco?*

I drop the journal back into the hiding spot beneath the floorboard and slowly lift my hands into the air. "Take it easy. I'm not going to put up a fight."

"I knew I should'a torched this place to the ground when I had the chance. I just figured that journal would be good insurance in case he ever decided to turn on me."

The southern twang of her voice is too distinctive to belong to anyone else. *"Carolyn?"*

"Stand up, darlin'. Nice and slow, now. Wouldn't want to hurt you after all you've been through."

"Where's Rocco?" I ask while doing as I'm told.

"Your hunk of a man is takin' a little snooze outside. He'll be alright. I just needed a minute of your undivided attention."

"You have it." I slowly turn around to face her. In a black velour tracksuit with the hood pulled over her platinum hair, she's nearly unrecognizable from the woman I met the day before. She could pass for a teenager on the street. The confident way she's gripping the pistol confirms what I had suspected earlier: her southern daddy probably taught her at an obscenely young age how to properly handle firearms.

"Why are you doing this, Carolyn?"

"I've spent forty-three goddamn years protectin' his dirty little secrets," she confesses, gritting her slightly crooked teeth. "That's almost the entire length of our marriage! Over four decades of eatin' shit and actin' like nothin' was wrong! You think I'm gonna let you just waltz into town and arrest him after all this time? The life I've built isn't over until I say so!"

"Bill killed Marianna," I assert with sickening clarity, pausing to digest the fact. On some level, I might share genetics with a murderer. "There may have been others, too. You don't have a lot of options at this point. What you're doing right this very minute is making you an accessory to murder. Do you comprehend what something like that would entail?"

She inclines her head. "Do you remember what happened that night? The night Marianna was killed?"

"No, but I don't remember much of anything that happened before we moved to Iowa," I admit. "I recognized Eddie, and I've had a few smaller flashes back into time. Nothing more."

"Good." Grinning, she braces her left hand beneath her right, taking direct aim at my heart. "That means once I've taken care of you and destroyed that godforsaken journal, no one else will know about Bill's involvement with Marianna. Of course, Diane was there, but she won't be tellin' a soul now, will she?"

I don't doubt she's a skilled marksman. The only way out of this is to keep her talking until I catch her at opportune time. "*Diane* was there that night?"

"She suspected ol' Frank was out here with Marianna, came here to confront him. Her daughter and Marianna's were sleepin' in the back of her car."

"What happened to Josephine?" I practically whisper. "Did Bill murder her, too?"

She looks away as her chest heaves with a sharp breath. Fat tears simultaneously slip down both cheeks when her gaze returns to mine. "It was an accident." She slightly lowers the gun when she sniffles. "Josephine was a sweet little thing...didn't deserve to have that happen. It came down to a matter of bad timin'."

I hold her gaze. "Does that mean I'm Lizzy?"

With a firm nod, she flicks a wrist over her tear-streaked face. "I *told* Bill you'd figure it out. I don't know why he insisted on carryin' on the charade that you're Josephine."

"Why did Diane and Frank take me and raise me as her?"

"By the time Diane found Josephine, it was too late to save her, and your momma was dead. She figured Bill was dead when she found him unconscious near the girls, so she grabbed you and fled. Diane told Frank she'd promised Marianna that she'd protect you, no matter the cost. They decided it was easier to pretend you were their daughter than explain the circumstances of that night."

A lump rises in my throat with the echo of Diane's last words. "She was protecting me from Bill."

"Damn straight. They were afraid he'd kill you, too." She sniffles again. "Little Josephine may not have had it comin', but your momma sure as hell did. After Bill knocked her up, she slept through the entire neighborhood—got involved with every married man in Federal Hill."

Sickness swells through me. "*Bill's* my father?"

"It sure as hell wasn't ol' Frank!"

"Because he's infertile."

"Diane never told a soul—one of the ladies from church overheard her talkin' with her doctor at the clinic when she was first pregnant. The identity of Josephine's real daddy died with Diane. Course it wouldn't surprise me one bit if Bill had fathered her, too." Her lips pucker as if she's eating something sour. "I would've left him as soon as I learned he'd gotten Marianna pregnant if it weren't for the oodles of money Bill had embezzled from that bank in Switzerland." Now smirking, she throws me a wink.

"Keepin' his little secrets made me a wealthy woman."

"By doing so, you've made yourself implicit in his crimes. And there's nothing *little* about cold-blooded murder." I point at the journal near my feet. "Have you read the things Marianna alleged he's done? Did you know about the Polaroid of a dead woman she found buried in his suitcase?"

Something sparks deep inside her gaze. I suspect it's guilt tinged with denial.

"You *do* know," I accuse her. "Were there more?"

She snarls her lip at the journal. "Hand me that. Those pictures, too."

I refuse to move. Once I give the items to her, it'll be game over. It's best to stall. Maybe Rocco will come around. *Please, God, let him be okay.*

"What're you going to do, Carolyn? Shoot me and leave me here for dead? I told the Baltimore PD everything I know about Bill and Marianna. They're aware this place exists." It's a bluff, but in hindsight I wish I had filled them in. "If you kill me, they'll find forensic evidence to put you away for the rest of your life. Do you know what they'd do to a pretty little thing like you in prison?"

"Stop talkin' like that. They won't find nothin' on me."

"You wouldn't say that if you'd ever worked a crime scene. There's always hair or fiber to be found. How are you going to explain your presence here?"

She closes her eyes and shakes her head. "You're lyin'."

"There's one thing I don't understand," I say, inching closer while her eyes remain closed. "Why did you knock Bill out when you realized I was coming to confront you about what Eddie claimed? If you're protecting Bill, why did you leave him behind and flee?"

Her eyelids pop open, revealing enlarged pupils. "You know what? I'm through with this nonsense." She raises the weapon. "Tell your daddy to rot in hell."

Before she can press it to her temple as intended, I spring forward to disarm her. The gun glides across the shack's floor as I tackle her onto her stomach.

"Stop!" she screams, kicking and thrashing her head. "Let me go!"

"Quit fighting me," I warn. "I'm twenty years younger than you. I can take a beating. You're only going to hurt yourself."

"What are you gonna do with me?" she shrieks. "You have no authority in this state!"

"I may not have the authority to arrest you, Carolyn, but I'm taking you in so someone else can."

———

On the short ride to the nearest police station in a town called Elkton, I make Rocco drive the rental while I ride in the back with Carolyn. He was in tough shape once I'd roused him and will need to see a doctor upon our return to the city. At least his head wasn't bleeding from the large rock she bashed against his skull. Still, I couldn't let him be responsible for Carolyn's detention. He's in no shape to fight anyone off, even if she is only a buck fifteen soaking wet. At the very least, I'm worried she'll try to throw herself into traffic.

She doesn't deserve a simple ending.

Without any zip ties or handcuffs available, I'd used the laces from Rocco's boots to bind her hands behind her back. Her pistol rests between my thigh and the door, easily accessible in case of an emergency. I've also activated the recorder on my phone. Although it won't be admissible in court, it may aid the Baltimore PD during their interrogation of Bill.

Ever since I practically stuffed Carolyn into the

car, she's been staring out the window with a blank expression.

"How long have you and Bill known about Marianna's journal?" I ask.

Her shrewd eyes dart over to me. "Diane and Frank sent a letter shortly after they'd moved away. Said they'd be keepin' a close eye on Bill, claimed they possessed hard evidence from Marianna regardin' the things he'd done. They even told their neighbor woman where to find it in case anything unfortunate happened to them."

Rocco's eyes meet mine in the rearview mirror.

Nonna.

"Why didn't they just turn Bill in?"

"They were using the diary as a kind of insurance. They threatened to hand it over to the authorities if he dared to come after Elizabeth or hurt another woman."

I'm oddly touched by my parents' actions and almost empathic to Diane's situation. Despite being bitter and cold-hearted, she was forced to raise the daughter of a woman who may or may not have been her husband's mistress. I don't know if I could've done something so noble.

I *do* know for certain that if I had been in their situation, I wouldn't have let a murderer walk free.

They should've turned the journal in when it fell into their possession.

"Did Bill stop hunting other women?" I ask.

Carolyn releases the smallest of smirks that doesn't reach her eyes. It's almost like she's sickened by the thought of him. "Matter of fact, he did. Stayed loyal to me after that, too."

"As far as *you* know," Rocco amends.

Carolyn purses her lips and returns her gaze to the window.

I can't shake the feeling that she's still omitting something important from her confession. Was she more involved in Marianna's death than she's willing to admit?

I stop the recording on my phone and blurt, "I killed Diane."

The tires on the rental screech as Rocco turns sharply around a corner. His gaze flickers to mine in the mirror, filled with endless questions. I give him a reassuring nod.

"You can't be serious," Carolyn says with an eye-roll.

I hold Rocco's stare as I continue my confession. "The morning she died...I ran outside to grab a scrunchie from my SUV. I was upset after crying all night and sat in the driver's seat, contemplating whether or not to hightail it back to school and never come back. Diane caught me in that vulnerable moment, said she was prepared to make my life a living hell if I didn't break up with the boy next door. She said I was embarrassing her and my father, and it wasn't right because he was so much older. I was confused when she told me that. I mean, we were only two years apart. Now that I know the truth, I know it's because, in reality, I was two years younger than what they'd brainwashed me to believe."

Rocco's complexion pales.

"But neither of us knew the truth then, so it didn't matter." I do my best to assure him everything's okay with a heartfelt smile. "I told her we were in love and planned to spend the rest of our lives together." I blink away the sting of building tears. "Wanna know what she told me in response to that?"

"What?" Rocco whispers, his eyes bright with pending tears.

"She said I was incapable of loving one man."

"She was comparin' you to your momma," Carolyn summarizes in a righteous lit.

"Of course, I didn't understand what she meant back then," I dismiss with a frail laugh, finally tearing my gaze away from Rocco's. "I was just furious that she would say something so cruel. After she left, I stewed for a while before I decided it was time to drag myself back inside. On the way out, my sweater caught on the gear stick. I felt it shift into neutral, but I was too worked up to give a damn. I remember thinking I hoped it would smash into the garage and wreck my parents' stupid house."

Carolyn lets out a cooing noise. "Ah, hun. Sounds like it was an accident. No need to beat yourself up over it."

"The police agreed it was an accident. Their investigation concluded a faulty gear stick on my SUV was to blame." I turn to face Carolyn with an eyebrow raised, hoping like hell I'm getting the message across because it's painful to pick at a wound that has taken decades to heal. "But I've always blamed myself for what happened. If I had given a damn...if I hadn't hated Diane so much... maybe she would still be alive."

Her eyes narrow. "Why are you telling me this?"

"Just something for you to think about. I imagine you'll have all the time in the world to reflect on your past and things you wish you would've done differently."

As we pull into the PD's parking lot, Rocco swipes an arm over his eyes. I do, too.

CHAPTER 22
BEFORE

Diane

The shack was easy enough to find. Marianna had explained its location well. The forest is dark and desolate, far enough from civilization that it would be a waste of time to cry for help.

I turn to find the girls still fast asleep in the backseat. They had passed out the minute we left the city limits. Elizabeth's head rests on Josephine's shoulder as she snores softly. They're wearing the matching pajamas Marianna made them for Josephine's birthday. Upon my daughter's insistence, I had braided their hair the same. They're so adorable, so pure, that I feel the weight of my decision to bring them along. It was a mistake. Hopefully it's not one I'll regret anytime soon.

But after Marianna had mentioned the damn shack in Elk Neck, I paged through the diary tucked inside Elizabeth's overnight bag. I had to see what's happening out here with my own eyes.

I have to know if Frank was the man Marianna had come here to meet.

As far as I know, my husband has never been unfaithful. But like the man in the diary, he's always on the road, selling encyclopedias. And he's been absent every weekend this summer, claiming to attend classes at an upstate university.

If the rumors about Marianna are to be believed, she has slept with every man in the neighborhood—including Frank.

It's time I confirm whether or not the rumors are true.

Soundlessly opening and closing the driver's door, I tiptoe the remaining distance between the car and the shack and gaze into the building's sole window.

There's a woman on the floor, unmoving. I'm

unable to see anything beyond a pool of blood and the woman's feet peeking out from a long wool skirt.

It's the same tan skirt Marianna was wearing when she left her daughter in my care.

I try to stifle my scream, but it's too late.

The door to the shack springs open, slamming against the side of the building.

I squeeze my eyes shut for a minute, certain I'm hallucinating.

"Bill?"

There's something primal in his gaze when my brother-in-law closes the distance between us. It's the purest form of evil I've ever witnessed.

I drag my gaze down to the object in his hand.

A bloodied knife.

Bill's dark gaze slides to something behind me. "What are they doing here? Why did you bring them?"

I turn to find Elizabeth huddled against my daughter in the doorway. At first, I assume they're hugging until I realize Josephine's eyes are fixed on the sight she's afforded through the open doorway. She's protecting her friend from the sight of her dead mother inside.

"Run, girls!" I cry to them. "Don't stop until you find help!"

Josephine's terror-filled eyes meet mine for a fleeting second before they sprint away.

Something sharp pierces my side. I cry out, crumpling to the shack's dirt floor with a blinding surge of pain. Then Bill's heavy footsteps fall in the same direction as the girls had gone.

"No," I pant, attempting to stand. A violent bout of nausea sends me down on my knees. "No," I wheeze before trying to rise once again.

I won't let that bastard hurt the girls.

I limp after them at a painstakingly slow rate, gripping my wound and wincing with every step. Although I lose track of them a time or two, I'm able to veer in the same direction as Bill's angry tirade.

"Come back here, girls!"

"I'm not going to hurt you!"

"Lizzy, do not disobey your father!"

I stumble with his last rant, barely bracing myself against a tree in time to prevent another fall. Bill is Elizabeth's father? Does Frank know? What about Carolyn? Does she suspect her husband has been having an affair? Is that why she spent so much time becoming involved in charities? How could she not know? They only live a handful of blocks down from Marianna.

With every bit of progress I make in their direction, my vision becomes mangled with black spots, and I become more light-headed. There's so much blood seeping from the wound that I know I won't be able to continue on for much longer. I'm close to losing consciousness.

A girl's scream pierces the air, followed by a man and woman shouting.

"*No*," I gasp as I collapse to the ground and close my eyes. "Not my baby girl…"

CHAPTER 23
PRESENT DAY

Josephine

On the other side of a two-way mirror, I watch Carolyn confess to knowing her husband's secrets. "He did it!" she cries, crushing a hankie in her hand. "Bill killed Marianna and Josephine, poor things! After all these years of hidin', it's a *relief* to say those words aloud! He threatened to kill me, too, if I came to the police! If it hadn't been for Lizzy bringin' me to my senses, I wouldn't have the freedom to tell you everything I know!"

Detective Frommie, a willowy man in his mid-30s

with a fat Tom Selleck mustache, leans over the interrogation table, relentlessly scowling. "What about the other women mentioned in Marianna Haley's diary? What do you know about them?"

Carolyn's fists pound at the table. "Nothing, I swear!"

His partner, Detective Carmichael, a petite woman with white-blond hair secured in a tight bun, sets her hand on top of Carolyn's. "I know this must be hard for you," she says in a warm, soothing voice. "But if you know *anything* about the other women that could enlighten us and steer us in the right direction, it would be extremely helpful. Names, locations of where he met them. Miss Haley claimed he took Polaroids of his victims. Have you ever come across any?"

Resting her forehead on the table, Carolyn sobs, *"I'm so sorry!"*

Captain Ruiz, the woman in charge of the detectives, switches off the speaker when Carolyn only continues to wail. Ruiz is stunning with an enviable bone structure, glowing brown skin, flawless black hair, and piercing eyes. Even without the 3-inch heels she's wearing, she'd still tower over my 5'9" frame. She omits an authoritative presence I'm able to appreciate.

"That's quite enough of that," she tells me in a sardonic tone. "I already sent two of my detectives to the hospital to take Bill Kelly into custody. They handcuffed him to the bed until the doctor finishes running a few more tests. I guess they're debating whether or not hip surgery is necessary."

Whatever causes him the most amount of pain, I think with a scowl.

I shake my head, frustrated. "Carolyn's still hiding something. She was ready to take herself out of the equation when I pushed her to explain why she left Bill behind. I think she's lying about what went down that night in the forest. I suspect she knows about the Polaroids, too."

"She's probably overwhelmed by shame," Captain Ruiz concludes. "All those years of living with a sociopath must've messed with her head." She crosses her arms and gives me a sly smile. "You did an excellent job here, Detective Kelly. If that diary is accurate, you've apprehended a serial killer with a higher victim count than Dahmer." She raises a lone, meticulously-shaped brow. "I don't suppose I can talk you into moving to Baltimore and working for me?"

"That *serial killer* may very well be my biological father," I remind her with a sharp look. "No offense, but I hope to never set foot in this city again."

"I guess I can understand that. I'm sure you'll be hearing from my department again in the near future —especially if they're able to uncover your birth mother's remains." She relaxes her shoulders with a sharp sigh. "Even once the FBI becomes involved, it'll be an arduous process of identifying whatever bodies we may or may not find buried on that property in Elk Neck." She offers her hand, and I shake it. "It's been a pleasure."

"Thank you for your cooperation, Captain Ruiz."

Her grip on my hand tightens before she releases it. "Wait, I almost forgot! You left your rental at the hospital and rode here in a squad car. Can one of my detectives give you a ride back?"

Remembering how I'd nearly cried when I was forced to leave Rocco behind for the doctors to examine, I dip my chin and smile. "That'd be great."

———

The detective drops me in the hospital parking lot. Rocco texts me, saying he's waiting in our rental car. I imagine he was eager to be released once they cleared him in the ER. Knowing him, he'd be embarrassed if his girlfriend saw him in a hospital gown.

My cheeks glow with warmth when I realize I consider myself his girlfriend. How's that going to work once I return to Chaska? He can't move away from Nonna. Would I be willing to leave the department in pursuit of something else? Could I return to Ames permanently, despite the decade of bitter memories that linger there? I briefly close my eyes and exhale. *One step at a time.*

I slip into the driver's seat beside Rocco and immediately lace my fingers through his. He ruffles his hair with his other hand and gives me a sheepish grin. Without any bandages, he would appear unscathed to a stranger. "How're you feeling?"

"Sore. The doc thinks I might be concussed. She said I'm clear to fly home, but I should take it easy for a day or two once we return." He gingerly leans the side of his head back against the passenger's seat. "It's mostly my ego that hurts. I can't believe I got knocked out by a senior citizen."

I bite down on a grin. "In your defense, she used a pretty big rock."

His fingers brush over mine. "I heard they arrested Bill for Marianna's murder."

"How?"

"There was a big commotion when the officers came. They'd stuck me in a hallway because the ER was so crowded, and I ended up right outside his room. I heard them read Bill his rights."

I glare at the monstrous brick building looming ahead. "A part of me wants to track him down in there and give him a piece of my mind."

His fingers tighten around mine. "What about the other parts?"

"I'm too exhausted to give a shit, Roc. Even if he truly is my birth father, he'll never mean anything more to me than a faceless sperm donor would." I reach for the steering wheel. "Let's pack our things and book the first flight back to Des Moines. I cannot wait to leave this city behind."

"You've always been one tough cookie." He lifts our combined hands to his mouth and brushes his lips over my knuckles. His expression intensifies. "That stuff you told Carolyn about the day Diane died—was that all true?"

"Every word," I ruefully admit.

"I hope you know by now what she said about you being incapable of loving one man was a load of shit. Especially when she never made an effort to know you the way I do." His Adam's apple skips over a lump before he continues. "When's the last time someone told you they loved you?"

Tears sting the back of my eyes. I quickly blink them away. "I have a few really good friends who tell me that every time we get together or speak on the phone."

He reaches out to tuck a wayward strand of hair behind my ear. His fingers linger against my jaw. "*I love you, Jo. I never stopped. You were always it for me.*" He leans his forehead against mine. "You can do whatever you want with that information, but I'm tired of holding back."

Although I'm closer to returning the sentiment than he probably realizes, I simply lean into him and accept the kiss he offers.

———

Two days later, I'm pleasantly surprised when I step into Noelle's office in downtown Ames. Her bedroom as a teenager had been grossly chaotic. Several decades later, her professional space is neat and orderly, with a rustic bookshelf and modern streamlined furniture in soothing shades of tan and gray.

"Josephine!" she squeals, jutting from behind a

glass desk to meet me in a steel-tight embrace. "My God, I've missed you!"

Laughing, I squeeze her back. "I've missed you, too. I just wish I was here under different circumstances."

Her chunky bracelets clang against her wrists when she releases me and draws back. I may not have recognized the stunning woman standing before me if I hadn't seen her hyphenated name on the door. Long, straight hair still as dark as a raven and skin as smooth as a 30-year-old's, no one would ever guess we graduated high school together. And, as I've recently learned, I'm biologically two years younger. After her third child, her hips remained slightly thick, and her breasts increased by two sizes —so she informed me one night years ago during a video call. She wears a black pencil skirt and a white turtle-neck sweater with tall boots with the ease of a seasoned supermodel.

"I'm glad Roc pressured you into coming," she admits. "You've been through quite the ordeal."

"You don't know the half of it."

Her smile drops. "I'd tell you I'm sorry to hear about your dad's passing, but I won't waste my condolences."

I nod in gratitude. The day after Bill's arrest, I

received a call from the nursing home. Frank had passed peacefully in his sleep. I felt nothing aside from immense relief. I won't have to endure another painful conversation with Frank ever again or pretend my childhood was normal.

She points a manicured finger at the chair facing her desk. "Have a seat."

Laughing nervously, I gesture to the leather couch in the corner. "Don't you want me to lay down on that?"

"Only if I truly believed it'd make you more comfortable." Snorting, she rolls her eyes. "I know you too well. You don't like feeling vulnerable."

"That's fair," I say, easing down into the chair facing her.

"Have you ever had any experience with hypnotherapy?" Noelle asks, her magnetic blue eyes skipping between mine. "There's no scientific evidence that it works, but it's yielded favorable results with a few patients in the past. It helped one survivor restructure their actual memories of abuse as a little girl." She folds her hands and sets them on the desk between us. "I can't guarantee whatever you come up with will be reliable, but it might jar something loose in that hard noggin of yours."

"If you truly believe it'll help..." I run my teeth

over my bottom lip. "You're not going to ask me anything inappropriate while I'm under, are you? I completely trust you in your professional capacity, but you did want me to tell you the details of what it was like to sleep with Rocco again."

"Nah. I'll save those questions for after we've had a few margaritas." She waves me away. "*Now* I need to you to lay on the couch. Relax as much as humanly possible."

Huffing, I follow her to the corner and spread out along the couch. Closing my eyes, I envision myself melting into the couch.

"I want you to pay attention to my voice," Noelle instructs me in a smooth, calming tone. "Niiiiiice and easy, Jo. I want you to go back into that forest in Maryland with me. Try to remember the sights, sounds, smells, thoughts, and feelings you experienced that night. There's nothing to be afraid of... we're in this together. We're in that forest alongside your friend. It's the night your birth mother was murdered."

I clear my mind, paying attention to my steady breaths as I imagine I'm back in the forest where we'd discovered the shack. Dense greenery, the scent of pine needles, the occasional sound of animals scurrying nearby. I focus my thoughts on the little girl in the Polaroid, pushing myself to remember the color of her eyes, the sound of her voice.

Beyond the darkness of my eyelids, the forest eventually comes into view. Chills zip over my skin. I squeeze the hand firmly clasped inside mine and look up to see the young girl with a brown braid wearing a nightgown.

"It's gonna be okay, Lizzy," she whispers.

Footsteps pound the ground behind us.

"He's chasing us," I wheeze, watching the forest stretch out before me with the clarity of a movie on a big screen. "There's a woman there, too."

"What does she look like?" Noelle prods.

"Her hair's yellow…like the sun. Her eyes are as blue as the ocean."

"That's good, Jo. You're doing great."

"She's holding a knife!" I whimper.

"It's okay, Jo. She can't hurt you. Not anymore."

"She's coming for him! She's raising the knife into the air!"

"This happened in the past, Jo. There's no need to be afraid. Do you know the woman?"

"Yes." In the playback, the man moves away from the yellow-haired woman.

A scream rips from my throat.

"Okay, Jo," Noelle says in a calm, firm tone. "Time to wake up now."

With a shudder, I open my eyes and look at my friend with desperation. *I can't comprehend what I just witnessed.*

"Who was that woman?" she whispers, reaching for my hand.

With a mournful shake of my head, I hop off the couch and head for the door.

"Talk to me, Jo!" Noelle pleads. "What did you see?"

On my way to the clinic's exit, I whiz past Rocco in the waiting room.

"Jo, wait!" he calls after me, jogging to catch up before I'm able to reach the doors. "What happened in there?" He captures my elbow in his grasp. "Where are you going?"

"My phone's in the car—I have to call Carolyn."

"Why?" His caring gaze sharpens. "What's going on?"

With my head cocked to one side, I briefly close my eyes. "I was right. She was lying about what went down that night."

CHAPTER 24
BEFORE

Carolyn

Once I arrive at the hideous shack in rural Elk Neck, my husband has already murdered Marianna Haley in cold blood. Although he's nowhere in sight and my sister-in-law's vehicle is parked in the yard nearby, I know it in my bones—Bill stabbed Marianna. I've suspected for over four years that his leisure pursuits are of the heinous variety.

My theory began when I discovered a Polaroid camera hidden on the top shelf of our bedroom closet. Once I'd replaced the film to see if it still worked, an obscene photograph of a woman that must've been stuck inside fell into my lap. Ironically, that same woman had recently moved into the rowhouse next to Frank and Diane's. Marianna was so cheerful and full of life in person that I had a hard time convincin' myself it was the same terrified model in Bill's Polaroid.

It was then I first realized there was nothin' ironic about Marianna Haley movin' into the neighborhood.

I cataloged Marianna's actions from afar for years after she moved into Federal Hill. The very first time I laid eyes on her, I sensed she was naive and malleable, like each and every one of Bill's prior whores. Somethin' about Marianna, however, was different. I couldn't put my finger on the reason until a few years later when I spotted her daughter playin' outside alongside my niece, Josephine. Other than their hair color, they could've been mistaken for sisters.

That's when I knew Bill had fathered Marianna's child.

Ever since I first learned of my husband's connection to the new woman in the neighborhood, I had increased my spendin' habits. Designer clothes, exotic vacations with friends, lavish parties at the clubhouse—nothin' was too expensive for a scorned wife. One way or another, I would make William Kelly pay for his sins against a former beauty queen. I could've been with any man of my choosin'. As fate would have it, I chose wrong.

Bill's muffled voice echoes through the chilled darkness. I'm unable to make out the words, only the furious intention behind them. Is he chasin' after Diane?

Fumblin' my way through the densely wooded forest, my eyes eventually catch on a glint of somethin' in the scant moonlight: a knife. I bend to snag the object by its handle, instantly nauseated by the smear of blood against the blade.

I married a monster.

It's time to make the evil bastard pay.

With the knife grasped firmly in my grip, I make it a few more yards when I come across a lump on the ground. I nearly pass it by, assumin' it's a dead animal of some kind until I catch a reedy moan.

"Diane?" I gasp, droppin' to my knees.

When she doesn't answer, I press my fingers against the side of her windpipe. A faint beat strains against my touch. Although she's alive, I check her for a wound and discover oodles of blood oozin' from her side. It seems Marianna wasn't Bill's only intended victim of the night.

"Lizzy, do not disobey your father!"

My heart slams to a stilted stop.

I'd invited Diane over for wine earlier in the night, but she'd declined, sayin' Josephine had invited the neighbor girl over for a slumber party.

My knees threaten to buckle.

Did Diane bring the girls along?

"I'll come back for you," I promise Diane, strokin' a hand over her clammy head. "I need to protect the girls."

Hot tears of fear and terror stream down my cheeks as I follow the direction of my husband's voice. If I had followed Diane when I'd first seen her car pull out of the driveway…would I have been able to stop Bill's murderous rampage? If he hurts those little girls, I'm not certain I can live with myself and my husband's actions.

When I spot Bill standin' in the clearin', I hold my breath and lunge at him, holdin' the knife out in front of me the way a knight would wield a sword.

By the time I realize my husband has leaped to the side, it's too late.

CHAPTER 25
PRESENT DAY

Josephine

know you killed Josephine," I tell Carolyn.

Her sharp gaze darts away from mine and lands on two little girls swinging across the park. A cold breeze passes through, and she shivers, lifting the lapels on her white pea coat. She doesn't confirm or deny my accusation. Her lips remain firmly pressed together as we sit in silence.

When I booked a return flight to Baltimore, I knew there was a chance Carolyn wouldn't agree to meet with me. The fact that she showed up at the time and place we agreed on makes me believe a part of her feels remorseful for her part in Bill's evil deeds.

"I remembered everything while in a therapy session," I explain. I set my hand on top of hers. "From my viewpoint, it looked like an accident."

"I've tirelessly replayed that night in my head ever since it happened," she confesses, her voice weak with pain. Tears brim her eyes as she continues. "Bill was my target. I found your momma and heard you girls cryin'. It was my intention to stop him before he hurt you, too. Had I known he was gonna move out of the way when he did…" Shaking her head, she removes an embroidered hanky from her coat pocket and dabs her eyes. "She was so brave, protectin' you from him." When she turns to give me a broken look, my heart gives a squeeze. "I hope you know I never would've intentionally hurt either one of you girls. Not in a million years."

"I believe you, Carolyn. I just wish you would've turned both yourself and Bill into the authorities back then. Not only was it the right thing to do, but it would've changed my life. You can't imagine how cruelly Frank and Diane treated me. I would've been better off in a foster home." I withdraw my hand and lean back, arms crossed. "What happened after

Josephine died? Did Diane really believe Bill was dead?"

"She didn't stick around long enough to find out," she admits with a slow shake of her head. "When Diane regained consciousness, she took you and left. Bill and I were too busy buryin' Jo and Marianna in a shallow grave to notice. He wanted to ensure I was just as invested in their murders and the coverup so I wouldn't go runnin' off to the police." She pauses with a fleeting glance that could almost be construed as an apology. "Have you told the detectives about this memory of yours?"

"Not yet. I wanted to talk with you first."

She squints. "About what?"

"The Baltimore PD and the FBI have been working overtime compiling a list of missing women who may have been Bill's victims, and attempting to locate their bodies in Elk Neck. Bill continues to deny any involvement with Marianna or any other women."

"I'm aware," she tells me with an irritated sigh. "His lawyer thinks he'll walk."

"You can't allow that to happen, Carolyn. You might be the only one who can provide them with irrefutable evidence linking Bill to those murders. The time to protect his secrets is over. I understand why you resent Marianna, but she was attempting to bring justice to his victims the night she lured him out to the shack. And she knew there was a good chance she'd die in the process." With a pleading look, I capture both of her hands in mine. "If there's *anything* you've been hiding, maybe receipts that would put him at the same location as those the missing women were last seen, anything unusual he's been collecting that might be trophies from his murders—"

"Those damn Polaroids," she murmurs.

Goosebumps spread across my skin. "Like the one Marianna mentioned in her journal?"

"Not exactly. The women are undoubtedly alive, but...they're all wearin' lingerie...some of them appear...uncomfortable."

My pulse throbs against my throat. "Where are they?"

She withdraws and rubs the palms of her hands against her thighs. "That depends. If I give them to you, are the police gonna charge me as an accessory to murder, like you said?"

I pause. I'm not an official part of the investigation and I don't know anything about the prosecutor on Bill's case. "If you hand the evidence over to the detectives, the state's attorney might request a shorter sentence. Maybe your attorney can even get them to set you up in a minimum security prison." Of course, I don't know if any of these things will happen, but I'm eager to sweeten the deal so she has a reason to cooperate. I squeeze her elbow. "Carolyn, you owe it to his victims. Their families deserve peace, once and for all."

With a resolved sigh, she begins digging through her designer handbag. Although the monitor on her ankle ensures she won't get too far without alerting the police, I'm not certain she doesn't own another handgun.

"What are you doing?" I ask.

"Lookin' for my phone. I'm calling my attorney. I'll have him meet me at the house before turnin' myself in. I'll let him decide the best way to handle the Polaroids."

As I exhale a long breath, a sense of peace settles over my bones. By the end of the day, I'll be reunited with Rocco and can begin to heal.

But there's one more stop I have to make on the way to the airport.

———

Tucked beneath a blanket on the hospital bed, Bill Kelly appears even more frail than he'd been when I found him unconscious on his patio. It wouldn't surprise me in the least if he's been starving himself in an attempt to convince a jury he's weak and harmless. I stand in the threshold to his room, carefully choosing the last words I'll ever say to the man who murdered my birth mother.

"Hello?" he calls out, his voice meek. "Who's there?"

"Cut the crap, Bill," I snap, moving in closer. "Recovering from a hip replacement at your age doesn't erase the fact that you're an evil monster." If I hadn't sworn to uphold the law, I'd be tempted to disconnect the IV pumping pain medicine into the back of his hand. "I only stopped by to let you know every little lie you've ever told is about to be exposed, and there's nothing you can do about it. Your victims...my birth mother...they'll finally have a voice."

His eyes harden. "Whatever it is you *think* you know—"

"I know everything, Bill. Your brother, Eddie, and your wife have agreed to testify against you." I lean down to whisper into his ear, "You're going to die in prison. And I hope it's as painful as hell."

As I step away to leave, he shouts, "Don't you walk away from me! How *dare* you disrespect your father this way!"

I shoot him a hateful look. "There's no proof that you're my father," I snarl, resisting the urge to slap him. "Marianna said so in her journal. And I have no desire to learn the truth, so I won't be taking a DNA test."

Swiftly exiting the room, a spark of satisfaction ignites in my belly when imagining a prison guard finding him shanked to death on a prison floor.

———

After I end the call with Captain Ruiz, I roll onto my other side to face Rocco with a quiet sigh. He's looking back at me with a devilish glint in his eye. Since I last returned to Ames, we've spent countless hours intertwined in his sheets. For the first time in my life, I have no desire to run from an intimate situation. There's nowhere else I'd rather be.

"They took Carolyn into custody after her attorney submitted the Polaroids," I tell him, watching my fingertip trail up and down his defined jaw. "She's being charged with involuntary manslaughter. Captain Ruiz believes they'll take her age into consideration and put her on house arrest."

"How does that make you feel?"

"Content, I suppose. I suggested they put Carolyn on suicide watch so she doesn't have the chance to end her shame."

"What did Captain Ruiz have to say about the Polaroids?"

"The FBI has already identified three women in the pictures who were reported as missing before Marianna's death. They've unearthed some human remains in Elk Neck, too. They're officially charging Bill Kelly with multiple counts of first-degree murder, including one for suffocating his own father in the nursing home."

"Jo, I'm sorry." He kisses my hand. "You realize none of this would've happened without you, right?"

"At least *something* positive came out of meeting my messed-up family," I agree with a snort.

"Now that you know your birth mother named you Elizabeth, are you still going to go by Josephine?"

"It feels wrong to change my identity after forty-nine—make that forty-*seven*—years. And my reputation as a detective hinges on that name. Besides, it seems fitting to honor the name of the brave little girl who saved my life."

"I couldn't agree more." He captures my lips in a lingering kiss before backing away with a nostalgic expression. "I've been putting this question off as long as possible: when are you headed back to Chaska?"

I briefly nibble on my bottom lip. "Would it freak you out if I told you I'm not? At least not permanently and not anytime in the near future. After I pack Frank and Diane's things and list the house, I'll have to do the same with my condo. With the proceeds from both sales, I should be able to afford something decent around here."

He rises to his crooked elbow. "Hold on. What are you saying?"

"Relax, big guy. I'm not proposing or anything." I push him down to his back and straddle him with a gleeful smile I can't contain. "But I *did* hand in my resignation. You can plan on seeing me around for as long as you'll have me."

"What if we looked for a new place together? It would be a fresh start for both of us...a break from our past. The day nurse thinks it's time to put Nonna in a memory care facility. As much as I liked growing up in this house, it's time to move on."

"I'd be open to the idea," I decide with a little thrill. A happily-ever-after with Rocco wasn't on my bingo card. Neither was discovering my birth mother had been murdered by the man who may have fathered me. "We *both* have a lot of mental trauma to sort through before things get too serious." I dust my fingertips over his wide lips. "Have you talked to the VA about your night terrors?"

"A lot of shit went down while I was in Iraq," he admits with a distant look. "I've stopped having nightmares since we left Baltimore, but I suppose it wouldn't hurt to properly address the issue with a therapist once and for all."

"Maybe Noelle can recommend someone who offers couples' discounts," I tease.

"Are you going to apply with the PD down here?"

"I don't think so." I heave a big breath and release a little smile. "The idea may be a little premature, but I'd really like to create a non-profit that advocates for abused women who don't think they have any options beyond staying in a toxic relationship."

"Like your birth mother."

"Like Marianna," I agree.

"This confirms my suspicion, Jo. You're the exact same person I first fell in love with." Gripping my wrists, he uses a classic wrestling move to roll me onto my back. His dark eyes bore into mine as he hovers above. "You know, starting a non-profit could take up oodles of your time. You'll be far too busy to properly take care of yourself. What if you had a built-in butler *and* chef who knew how to make the world's best tortellini in brodo?"

"You have my attention." Smirking, I quirk one brow. "Is this theoretical butler good-looking?"

"Looks are subject to every individual's personal taste," he recites with ease. He lowers down to brush his lips over mine. "But I'm pretty confident you'd be attracted to this one."

"Could that butler also draw me a bubble bath at the end of the day and ensure I'm properly tucked in at bedtime?"

"Define *properly*."

Henry hurdles the bed and lands between us. He lets out a happy bark and spins in a circle before eagerly licking Rocco's face.

"I think he approves of our plan," I tell Rocco, giggling as he attempts to dodge the dog's wayward tongue.

He finally wrestles Henry down to his stomach where he happy accepts a scratch on his belly. "This guy needs a big house in the country with several acres to properly burn up all his energy. Maybe we could adopt another dog after we return to keep him company."

"After we return?" I repeat. "Where are we going?"

"Somewhere far away where you can recharge and relax before all this packing business begins. Maybe somewhere involving cliffs and the ocean...or the sea."

I sigh happily. "That sounds amazing."

His lips dust over mine before quirking with a grin. "You don't know it yet, but while we're there, I'm going to convince you to become my wife. Maybe you'll even agree to marry me on one of those cliffs."

I part my lips, intending to tell him any "convincing" on his part isn't necessary, but he silences me with a kiss.

I'm done fighting my feelings for Rocco Giordano. As a teenager I was convinced I would marry him, so it's about time we make it happen. He's the only family I could ever want and the only one I'll ever acknowledge.

ABOUT THE AUTHOR

With over 40 captivating titles spanning various genres, Quinn Avery first honed her talent for crafting intricate puzzles through her smart and quirky Bexley Squires mystery series. Her contemporary suspense thrillers, often set in her beloved locales such as Mankato and Lake Shetek, are nothing short of addictive, leaving readers spellbound with their mind-spinning twists. When Quinn and her husband aren't off on adventures, they enjoy the tranquility of their Minnesota acreage and lake home in their newfound empty-nest phase.

For more information, visit www.QuinnAvery.com.

ACKNOWLEDGMENTS

Big shout-out to Najla Qamber and her team for creating this stunning cover! Your crew is always patient with me and knows exactly what I prefer. 🤍

Thank you to DeDe Kelly for being a great friend and one of my biggest supporters (in addition to being badass). So glad fate brought us together!

Thank you to Christy Freeberg for your unwavering excitement over my work, no matter what state it's in! You're the best! 🤍

Thank you to every last reader who has purchased my books and has shown unwavering support of my career - especially the Instagram bloggers who promoted *Right Across the Bay*, and my Blue Earth Area and Lake Shetek fans! It means a lot knowing the locals have my back and enjoy my work!

Most of all, thank you to my family for always being there and putting up with my insanity. Especially my husband, my soulmate…without you, none of this would be possible.